GOLD MINE

SKYE WARREN

CHAPTER ONE

ADAM

THE MANSION GLOWS like a goddamn castle. Yellow light glows from every window, reflecting onto the moat that surrounds the modern fortress. I want dark shadows and bloodshed.

Instead I'm given glaring light and champagne.

I step carefully onto the rickety pile of wood they're calling a boat for the crossing. A man dressed in old-world gondolier clothing stands at one end, wielding a long stick. "Hello, my fine friend," he says in Italian. "How goes your night so far?"

Bullets flying would be preferable to this. *Water.* Not my favorite. "*Bene.*"

He steers us gently across the twenty-foot-wide space, not being especially fast about it. I suppose he's hoping for a large tip at the end of my ride. "Do you look forward to the food? The drink? The beautiful women?" He laughs. "They are very beautiful tonight."

"Yes," I say, my voice grim. He's correct about that, I'm sure.

There's only one beautiful woman I'm concerned about.

We pass under a bridge made of stone. It would have been far easier to walk across it, but it's closed for the evening. And I'm not playing the part of a person who would scale the wall. I'm not playing the part of a thief or a criminal. Instead I'm playing myself. Adam Black. A man born to an empty legacy. A hollow dream. Money and nothing else.

The boatman lingers only a few feet away from the landing dock, and I grit my teeth against the urge to make the jump. Adam Black wouldn't do that. My true identity would recline for the ride, looking forward to the food and drink and women. And a few less legal vices.

"Is it your first time visiting the Castello del Esposito?" he asks.

I was here once as part of a raid for stolen artwork. And another time, I stole through the roof to break into their jewel safe. Two sides of the same coin.

In both cases I took what was not mine. Power. It's addictive. And draining.

"*Si*," I say, because Adam Black has never been here.

In a sea full of billionaires and crime lords, I hand over a tip that will be his best tip of the night. I need all the friends I can get for what I'm about to do. I leave him singing his thanks to me and enter the receiving line. I'm checked at the door. Not for weapons. Almost every man in the place will be armed. And many of the women, too. No, they want to see my passport. They could spot a fake a million miles away. It's my real passport that I give them. Adam Black. American citizen. Well traveled, but never to places with war and famine.

They wave me through.

In the main ballroom the event has reached its pinnacle. Men and women swarm the parquet floor, fabric rushing, skin sweating. Laughter spirals to the gold-plated ceiling.

I scan the grinning, wild-eyed faces for one in particular.

And I find her. *Almost.*

She has the same curve of her cheek. The same turn of her shoulder. The same blonde and honey-colored hair, only a little lighter with artificial highlights. She's not the woman I seek.

That's what I tell myself, anyway. That I didn't come here for her.

She's Holly's sister, which means she'll lead me to her.

London stands toward the back of the room, her lips pressed together in a sharp line. She's worried, which means the game has already started.

A man approaches her, and I know immediately what he wants.

I stroll up quickly, my movements exaggerated. In this game I'm drunk and entitled. And powerful. I put my hands on her shoulders and bring her in for a kiss on each cheek. "Darling. I've missed you. It's been too long since I've had your sweet company."

She looks bewildered for a moment. The half-mask I'm wearing, I suppose.

Then her eyes widen. She tries to back away from me, because she thinks I'm the most dangerous man in the room. That might be true, but I won't hurt her. Because it would make Holly sad. So I force her onto the dance floor, my grip uncompromising.

"Darling," I say, warning in my voice as she stands there.

With stiff movements she puts her arms on

me and allows me to lead. We move with the heavy, seething motion of the crowd, an almost frantic edge to the antiquated waltz.

"What are you doing here?" she says, her voice low and panicked.

"I'm here to protect you," I say in a mocking tone.

She yanks her arm, but I don't let go. "Get away from me. And my sister."

"I'm afraid I can't do that. Now, is she already talking to that bastard Taggart? And where did he take her?" *And why are you here alone? Why are you so goddamn breakable?*

I could break you.

Worry bleeds into London's pretty blue eyes. "He was dancing with her. I was watching them, and then suddenly, it happened so fast, they were gone."

"Where did you last see her?"

She points to a corner of the dance floor. I know for a fact that the corridor entrance is right behind there, leading to dark antechambers for people to fuck or use drugs. Or in this case, conduct an illegal exchange of diamonds.

"Good. I'll find her."

"Please." Her lips tremble, and if I were an ordinary man, I would find it delicious. It would be a pleasure to make her tremble for another reason. Instead I'm perverse. I want to bite her lips. I want to watch them bleed. I hurt anyone that I come near, which is why I'm determined to stay away. I've come just long enough to save her, to save her sister. To make amends.

And then I'll leave Italy.

Her sister is in love with Elijah North. He can't be far behind me.

And wherever Elijah goes, Lieutenant Colonel Mark Jefferson is not far behind.

"There's one thing I need you to do for me. Dance with the men. The ones who look the most dangerous. Keep them interested. And stay at the center of the crowd."

"What? Why?"

"Because that man wanted to take you somewhere dark." And despite my very best intentions, I've become the reluctant defender of the Frank siblings. "Most likely he would have been given instructions not to harm you, but you can never be sure. And most men of his kind don't consider a few stolen kisses to be harm."

I should know. I used to be a man like that. *Too late.*

"Okay," London says, her voice shaky. She really is gorgeous. The kind of delicate, wide-eyed beauty that will make men fall over themselves to dance with her. To save her from herself.

Unfortunately I'm only interested in ruining her.

I take a step back as the waltz ends and give her a small bow. "*Addio.*"

CHAPTER TWO

HOLLY

Five minutes earlier

HEAVY FOLIAGE CREATES the illusion of a jungle.

Each leaf has been painted a matte or glossy black, with the rare pop of metallic gold. That's the color theme for the event. The ballroom overflows with black silk and gold jewelry in every arrangement imaginable. There's only the rare pop of white—a dress shirt, a string of pearls. Gleaming white teeth in a too-large smile.

Dread creeps over my skin, and I shake out my glittering skirts in a nervous gesture. The more boisterous the crowd becomes, the more I regret coming here.

It was not really a choice.

A waiter passes by with a gold serving plate full of champagne. I swipe a flute and drink down the bubbly liquid too fast. Air tickles my nose. I cough until my eyes tear up.

Something rustles the plants behind me, and I jump.

Is it them? Is it time? A couple emerges from black-painted leaves, stumbling over their own feet, laughing, the woman's dress askew, the man's bow tie undone.

They disappear into the crowd.

Pain lances my palm. I look down to see that I've crushed the champagne flute in my hand. The glass sliced through my skin. A thin line of red mars the austere color scheme of the event.

My sister appears with a white linen napkin. She swipes at my hand, her movements rough and uneven. "You need to relax," London mutters, sounding shaky herself.

"We should go," I whisper, trying and failing to keep my voice even.

"Go? We haven't done what we came here to do."

"We're going to make an exchange of illegal goods at the most crowded place in the world? Why did we ever agree to this? This is a terrible idea."

"Don't go supersonic."

"I'm not going supersonic." Deep breath. "Okay. *Okay.* I'm serious though. What if they aren't going to show up? Or what if this is a trap?"

"Set by who? The diamond police?"

A man appears at my side. The women here wear elaborate masks in every color and fabric that match their gowns. Mine is gold. London's is silver. Meanwhile the men primarily wear black to match their tuxes. This is one of the rare exceptions. He wears one of those masks with long noses, the kind that remind me of the plague. Instead of being black and dreary, his is white and embroidered with gold thread. The joviality of the colors combined with the grimness of the shape sends a shiver down my spine.

"Hello to two beautiful ladies," he says with a slight bow. "May I have this dance?"

"No, thank you," I answer for both of us.

The man gives a slight smile, as if I've said something clever, a joke that we're both in on. "Now I know with whom I must dance. It's you, of course. The leader."

My eyes narrow from behind my glittering mask. "No means no."

"I think you want to dance with me. In fact, I think you came here expressly for this purpose."

A slight gasp from beside me. My sister knows what I've suspected. This is the man who's supposed to make contact with us. "Perhaps we can go somewhere more private?"

He makes a tsk sound. "And skip the foreplay? I think not."

He holds out his arm, and I take it with great reluctance. It feels a little like taking the scaly arm of an alligator, one who's already showing me his hundreds of teeth.

A waltz begins, and he sweeps me into a smooth arc. The man can dance, I'll give him that much. He may be an international thug, one who threatens my sister, but he's a skilled dancer. He leads me with such effortless skill, it almost feels like floating.

"Call me old-fashioned," I say, "but shouldn't we conduct illegal business somewhere where there aren't a thousand other people?"

He glances down my body, to my cleavage. My skin crawls. "Oh, we will. Right now I'm having a good time imagining all the places you might have hidden the diamonds."

"Maybe my sister has them."

"No," he says decisively. "It's my business to know who has the power. It's you."

"It's us," I say, correcting him. "We have what you want."

He grins, showing a gleaming white smile beneath the long nose of the mask. "I know, sweet thing. I do know that. That's why I haven't killed her yet."

I stiffen in his arms, almost stumbling to a halt amid the whirl of other couples. "Don't you touch her. Don't you touch a hair on her head or I swear to God I'll—"

"Calm down, calm down. I have no intention of hurting her. All I want is the money she owes me. You seem to be in some doubt as to my role here. I'm a businessman, first and foremost."

"I know exactly what you are." A loan shark.

"Good." His hands tighten. "Then there won't be any tricks tonight."

"No tricks." It will be a relief to give up the diamonds, actually. They've become heavier with every day that's passed, gained a thousand pounds of emotional weight with every month. So heavy that dragging them around makes my muscles sore, even if it's only in my head. Every day has taken us farther away from Elijah, and each day has broken something inside me.

He nods once, decisive. Ian Taggart has a reputation that even I've heard about in my insulated American experience. An international loan shark with dangerous tactics. More than one of his competitors have disappeared.

Without missing a beat, he sweeps us out of the flow of dancing couples.

Two men appear out of nowhere in plain black masks and large builds.

They surround me on either side, forming a human cage. I glance back, wild-eyed, for my sister, but there's only a whirl of black and red and gold.

"Don't worry," the man says, reading my mind. "You'll return to her shortly, once you and I have finished conducting our business."

The way the words roll off his tongue, it sounds as if we're going to meet for a private affair, rather than a cold, violent business deal. Then again, that's probably what everyone thinks as I enter one of the antechambers. There's not only one man with me. There's three. What must people think of me? A slightly hysterical laugh bubbles up.

Then we're alone, the sound of the waltz abruptly muted, and my laughter disappears.

Shadows reign in the lush antechamber. They patrol the perimeter of the room. They lean on the armchairs and tables. The man sits on an oversized sofa, one arm slung over the back, his legs spread. He whips off the plague mask, revealing handsome features and a cold expression.

He's clearly the king in this scenario, and I'm

his subject.

I lift my chin and take a step forward. "So, let's do business."

Another slow glance over my breasts, my waist, my hips. It makes me feel naked instead of encased in gold satin. "You show me yours, and I'll show you mine."

I lean down to pull something out of my petticoat. A small black velvet pouch holding a single diamond. I toss it to him. He catches it deftly and tips the gem onto his palm. "Seems real enough. Worth maybe ten thousand dollars. Not even close to the five hundred thousand your sister owes me."

"I have the rest. Once I get your promise that she's safe."

"I've already told you I have no interest in hurting her."

"And once I get your promise that you won't loan her any more money."

That earns me a dark laugh. "You drive a hard bargain."

"Your word?"

"You understand that I could break my promise."

"It's possible."

"And you understand that I could tear that

pretty dress from your curves and retrieve the diamonds myself. I wouldn't mind doing a full-body search."

I struggle to hide my shiver. "That's also possible. I'm hoping you behave honorably."

"God. When's the last time someone expected me to behave honorably?" He glances at one of his muscle-bound men in tuxes, as if they might have the answer, but they stand there stone-faced, still in their plain black masks. "Fine. You have my promise."

"On both counts."

"On both counts. Though you should know that I'm not the only person she borrowed money from. Nor am I the most ruthless. Your sister has a slight drug problem."

It's my problem now. I won't let her face this alone. She's been doing well enough without the drugs—though in a sudden flash of insight, I realize she might be procuring them when she goes on walks. She needs a real rehab center, not a string of hostel beds.

That's something to figure out later. The deal here is complete. Any other debts will have to wait for another day. I reach down to pull out the rest of the diamonds. I'm bent over, exposed, defenseless, when I hear the cock of a gun.

CHAPTER THREE

HOLLY

ADAM FACES THE four of us with a pistol in his hand, no fear in his cold gray eyes. He looks taller than I remember him, stronger than I remember. "You're under arrest."

The two men on either side of Ian Taggart already have their weapons drawn. They point at Adam. Adam points at them. We have a standoff, and I'm right in the middle.

Ian Taggart speaks in rapid Italian. "Are you AISE?"

"Interpol."

"He's not really Interpol," I say. "He's corrupt."

"You know him?" Ian's eyes narrow on me. "You fucking *brought* him?"

"No! I swear! I had no idea he was even here."

Ian stands, as calmly as if there were no fingers on triggers in the room. I wonder if I'll ever have his casual self-possession in the face of imminent death. If I have any more dealings with Adam and Elijah, it just might happen. Either that or they'll make me insane.

"I'll take this as interest," he says, holding up the small diamond to the low light. The light refracts in even the tiny surfaces, showering glitter across my gold dress. "And you can be assured I'll be back to collect the full payment."

"Where do you think you're going?" Adam asks.

"Back to the party. Unless you want her pretty dress splattered with blood."

Then Ian strolls out of the room, the two men following, their guns trained on me until the last possible moment. I whip around to see Adam put his gun away, looking fierce, a warrior thwarted. "Hell," he says. "How did you get mixed up with that thug?"

I glare at him. "And you're so much better than him."

He gives a short laugh. And then inclines his head as if conceding the point. "I agree that you haven't seen me in exactly the best light."

"Kidnapping can do that."

"I came here tonight to help you."

"Well, you didn't. I was about to pay off a man who's been threatening my sister."

"Using stolen property."

"You mean the diamonds? Of course you mean the diamonds." I have to admit, if only to myself, that I'm disappointed it was Adam who found me. Adam, the man who entangled me in this terrible business. Not Elijah, the man who saved me. "You want them."

"Yes. I want them. A lot of people want them."

Frustration feels like boiling water beneath my skin. "You could have them, you know. I don't care about them. No, it's worse than that. I hate them. I despise them. Why someone is making such a fuss over rocks, I have no idea."

"Why do I get the feeling you're not about to hand them over?"

"I need them. I need them for my sister."

"Your sister."

I stride across the room to the door, and the party blinds me anew with its color and light and sound. "She's probably looking for me. Worried about me."

"Or she's dancing with a stranger."

The words pierce my secret worry, that I'm not important after all, that I'm too insignificant, too *strange* to really care about. I've turned my life upside down to go on the run with her. Would she do the same for me? I shake my head. Of course she would. We're sisters. This man is trying to divide us. For what purpose? To take the diamonds. Though I couldn't say why he doesn't kidnap me again. Instead he lets me walk into the ballroom, following a few feet behind. For a moment there's only a wild kaleidoscope of color. Then it focuses, and I see my sister standing where I left her, her hands clenched together so tight her knuckles are white, her blue eyes frantic. She sees me a second later, and relief floods her. God, I'm such a fool for doubting her—even for a second. We're *sisters*. A bond like that can never be broken.

I rush toward her, and she toward me. We meet along the back of the room, near the black and gold foliage. In unspoken agreement we wait until we're neatly tucked behind a heavy fern before speaking. "What happened?" she demands.

"Were you in danger?" I have to know that first. "He said he had men watching you. He said—"

"No." Her gaze moves behind me, and I know Adam has followed us. "He found me first. He told me to keep dancing, to keep moving, that they wouldn't touch me as long as I was with someone else."

Relief fills me. "Thank God for that."

"But then it took so long, and the men here are jacked on more than just alcohol, so it took so much effort to keep them from being grabby. Did you make the exchange?"

I glance back at Adam. "No."

Something stops me from blaming him in front of my sister. Some niggling suspicion that maybe this needed to happen. That he really did save us tonight.

"You're thinking of Elijah North," he says. "Wishing I were him."

"No," I lie.

"You shouldn't trust him."

"God, you've said that to me already. But you know, he isn't the one who put a black hood over my head. He isn't the one who threw me into a white van."

"No. I did that."

There's regret in his eyes. Or maybe that's just a trick of the flickering candles. Either way I can't believe it. I learned not to trust Elijah, but I also learned not to trust Adam. It's a dark game they play. One I don't want to be in the middle of.

"Enough," he says, his voice low. "They might come back. We need to be gone."

"Where are we going?"

He gives me a small smile, almost bittersweet. "Oh, we're not going anywhere. You're going somewhere you'll be safe. Only I won't be joining you."

I don't have time to ask what he means. He's pushing through the crowd, creating a small river for us to follow him. I grab my sister by the wrist and take off after him.

Maybe it's insanity. Or a suicide wish. This man hurt me once, badly. In the worst way a man can a woman, but he feels like a lifeline here.

In a sea of monsters, he's the most dangerous.

We reach the outside, where the gondolas ferry people back and forth over the moat. Something has already gone wrong here. A single gondola floats aimlessly, empty, its oar a couple yards away. The men in white dress shirts manning the valet station have disappeared. Worry rises in my throat. How could I have made it out of here alive? My sister squeezes my hand, and I resolve that we'll make it. It's a pure force of will.

A loud bang comes from around the side of the mansion, and we jump. Adam puts his body in front of mine, his hand on my arm, keeping me back. Keeping me safe.

Shadows split apart. A man appears. It must

be my imagination. He can't really be here, after so many months of running. Then again, it feels inevitable. Every day I ran away from him, I was also running toward him.

"Elijah," I manage to say, relieved my voice doesn't waver.

"Did he hurt you?" he asks. Even in the moonlight his eyes glint a beautiful, brilliant green. He's an otherworld creature, all the more powerful in the night.

"No. He protected me, actually. He—"

"Don't touch her," he says, his eyes flashing to the man in front of me. After a brief moment of tension, Adam steps aside. "He wasn't protecting you."

"No, really. He—"

"Don't worry about it," Adam murmurs to me. "I do have a way of bringing the two of you together, don't I? Perhaps one of these days you'll thank me for it."

"Don't touch her," Elijah says again. "Don't talk to her."

"Then I'll take myself someplace else." A small bow. "North. Until we meet again."

A growl sound escapes Elijah, and I realize he isn't dressed like Adam. He's not wearing a tux. Not attired for the gala. Instead he's wearing all black. A T-shirt and combat pants. Boots. He looks like he's going into battle. "He's only after the diamonds."

I roll my eyes. "You think I don't know that? You think I'm confused, and that he came all the way to Italy to tell me my eyes are pretty?"

"He said that to you?"

"He was lying," I say, my voice flat. "The same way you are."

"I'm lying to you," he says, soft and dangerous. "I've barely even said anything."

"Even you being here is a lie. Pretending you care who touches me, who hurts me. The black SUV you drove was a lot nicer than the white van, but the result was the same."

"You were never my prisoner."

"Then you shouldn't be upset that I left."

He makes that growl sound again, and my sister moves to stand in front of me. "You don't want Adam to talk to her?" she says. "You don't want him to touch her? That's fine with me. Then you don't get to touch her, either. Both of you are fucked up. Both of you are dangerous."

I tense, expecting Elijah to say something sharp.

Or maybe even throw my sister bodily out of the way.

He seems like something feral right now. A beast who's been denied his meal for far too long. Except he blinks and takes a step back. His eyes turn to a muted, cool green. "Then get in the fucking boat. Don't cause any trouble, and I won't have to touch you."

It's a sign of her self-preservation that she steps into the small gondola.

I follow close behind.

I have no doubt that Elijah would manhandle me into the boat if I refused. And for once, I'm not interested in fighting him. It was too terrifying being in a standoff between an international criminal and a dishonest Interpol agent. I need some peace, even if it comes in the form of Elijah North, with all his demons and his secrets.

CHAPTER FOUR

ELIJAH

A YEAR AGO I was given an assignment. Infiltrate a ring of arms dealers and intercept their payment in the form of diamonds. It was there that I found Holly Frank, a frightened hostage. My fellow cellmate. It was there that I broke into a thousand pieces.

A year ago…

My mission fell to shit, and the worst part is, I didn't care.

The only thing I wanted was to keep her safe. I threw away my career, my rank, my reputation, on this slip of a woman with messy hair and wide brown eyes.

Then she left me, and I lost my goddamn mind.

Three hundred and sixty-seven days of searching for her.

Now she's sitting in a boat that's painted black and gold as I row us across the water. It isn't a romantic moment. Her back is stiff. Her sister glares at me. Too fucking bad. She's going to have to get used to me. They both are.

We reach the dock, and I help both of them out. It's a parody of chivalry. I'm no gentleman. Never have been, and the past few months have cut me too close to the bone.

There's an entire goddamn army of men waiting for us.

Thankfully, they're on our side.

I meet my brother Liam in a two-handed clasp.

"All clear?" he asks.

We expected some resistance. "We had company. Adam got there first."

Liam swears. "You shoot him?"

"Not this time." He protected Holly in there, and for that he got a pass. But I owe him a bullet in exactly the same place where he shot me a year ago. One day soon.

Liam wanted to come with me into Castello del Esposito, but I didn't let him. Bad enough that he's risking his entire security company to help me get away. I wasn't also going to let him get charged with a crime if things went sideways.

"Take London," I say, my voice low.

My brother gives me a sharp look. We weren't

close growing up. He got the hell out of our abusive house as soon as he could enlist, and I never blamed him for that. We're close now, though. Getting closer, especially when he can read my goddamn mind. "You have some things to discuss with Holland Frank?"

"A few."

"Do I need to send someone to keep her safe?"

I bare my teeth. Brother or not, no one's getting between us. "You could try."

He studies my eyes, his own dark and thoughtful. What does he see? Our father was a violent bastard who killed our mother. He used to beat Liam until he was half-dead, claiming he was beating the devil out of him. Ironic, really. I was the only who grew up with the devil inside him. And I stared at my father in the same green eyes when I killed him.

Should he leave Holly alone with me? No one should trust me with a goddamn flower pot, but it's going to happen. I've been waiting too long for her.

Whatever Liam sees, it makes him nod.

Then he's shepherding London Frank into the SUV ahead of us and closing the door behind them. Holly looks at me, her mask askew, the heavy weight of her upswept hair falling down around her shoulders. She looks like a princess whose carriage has turned into a pumpkin. This isn't the story of how she's found by a prince. This is the story of the highwayman who finds her on the side of the road and has his way with her.

Despite the fervor of my blood, I find myself gentle as I take her by the waist and guide her to the black SUV in the back of the cavalcade.

When I open the door, she looks up at me, her eyes deep wells of sadness and worry. "I'm not sorry I left," she says, though it sounds like an apology.

"I know," I say, my voice soft.

"Are you still very angry about it?"

"Furious," I say, my voice casual. "I plan to take it out on your pretty little body."

That gives her pause. She stills in my hold like an animal scenting the air, scenting danger. She should know that I'll hurt her. It's inevitable. As inevitable as finding her.

She's my prey, and I'm her monster.

The tinny sound of a voice from the front signals the start of our journey, and the SUV rolls forward. I can feel the caution in the way the vehicle moves, sense the strategy in the path we take. We're in good hands right now. Safe right now, which is the only reason I roll up the divider between the front.

Holly looks at me, wariness in her sweet brown eyes.

Good.

I drag her onto my lap, ignoring her whimper of surprise. God, she's so soft and perfect in my arms. A little slimmer from life on the run, but still plenty soft in the places I need. I long to press my palm against the weight of her breast, to nudge her ass with my hard cock.

I could even make her want it. Call it gratitude, call it an adrenaline response. She could be warm and lush around my cock as we bump over roads hundreds of years old.

That's not what she needs, though.

"I'm sorry," she says, her voice trembling. "I don't—know why—I'm doing this."

The same chemicals that would have made her pussy wet are making her do this.

A normal response to being in a life-or-death situation. The only thing to do after is fight or fuck. Or if you're a beautiful woman, both strong and fragile, you cry.

The realization is like a gut punch. She's going to cry. There's nothing I can do to stop it.

"Let it out," I say, no softness in me whatsoever. There's only iron in my arms as I hold her, ice in my heart as she fights those hot tears glistening in her eyes.

"Why did you—"

Why did I follow her? Because I can't sleep or fuck or breathe when she's not near me. I need her, and I resent that fact even as I acknowledge its finality.

She sucks in another shaky breath. "Why did you take so long?"

It's a bullet in the brain. A killing blow, the knowledge that she must have been scared, that she must have been goddamn terrified to want me. *Me.* "I'm sorry," I say roughly, meaning it. God, it's one of the only honest things I've said. "I'm sorry it took me so long."

An eternity, and she spills out every second we were apart in saltwater. Tears leave glittering tracks down her cheeks. They land in fat drops on my arm. I squeeze her tight, as if I can apologize for the time with pressure, with pain.

"I was so afraid," she gasps, sobs wracking her body.

"I know. The gun. That bastard Taggart."

"He said he had my sister."

She will tear herself apart trying to save her sister. "He had *you.*"

"And then Adam showed up with a gun, and I

thought…" Her voice breaks. "I kept thinking you would be too late, and that you'd feel guilty."

I'm not sure it's possible for me to sink farther tonight. I'm lower than dirt, than clay, than molten tectonic plates. She will tear herself apart trying to save *me*. "You're so damn worried about other people when a gun's pointing right at you, sweetheart."

She cries for an hour, each tear drawing a line across my heart, my private penance for failing to be there a minute early, a month earlier. An eternity earlier.

That's me, though. My curse, always to be too late.

Finally her tears quiet. She looks at me, curious. "Were you worried about me?"

Was I worried? She must not be able to see the shadows under my eyes. The edge of frantic worry that kept me awake as I wondered where, where, where. "A little."

"How did you find me anyway?"

I don't really want to tell her. Partly because it gives away my edge. If she escapes again, she'll hide the same way. And partly because it exposes too much about her. About me. "I read your book. The one about the tooth fairy."

"I told you that story."

"You told me about how she became fascinated with humans. How she went to visit one boy in his room, but he was sick. Terminal. And he died. You didn't tell me the story ended there."

"It did," she says on a sigh. "Readers were so angry, but it had to end that way."

Once upon a time we were trapped in a prison together. She told me about her work as an author. She didn't tell me that she was world renowned, with photos of her in signings around the world, smiling teenage girls holding up their fan art.

She didn't tell me that reading her books would be a window into her soul.

"I read the sequel."

She scrunches her nose. "You did?"

"I did."

Twelve months after she disappeared from my apartment, another book was published. This one was sent digitally to her publisher from an anonymous device. A sequel to the tooth fairy book, titled *After You Left.*

I used every contact, every resource, every goddamn method of finding someone, but she was untraceable. Disappeared. In my darker moments, I was afraid that she had died. That's why I couldn't find her. She was buried at the bottom of a lake somewhere, like my mother.

Then the book came out, and I read about how the tooth fairy, expelled from her community of other fairies, heartbroken from losing her only human friend, wandered the world. She sold handmade trinkets for cash from tourists, acting always as the native, even though she never belonged. Never belonged anywhere, really. Cash. Trinkets are a cash business, and she paid for her purchases the same way. A coastal town. Some references to an Italian church.

It had been enough for me to finally find her.

The SUV bumps along at an incline, and I know we're beginning the long climb up the Amalfi coast. There was enough time between reading the book and finding her for me to purchase a small house. A small fortress. It overlooks an expanse of blue—the ocean, the sky. Hardly any land. Sometimes I think she'll like the lemon trees in the yard. Other times I imagine her beating herself against the confines of the cage, breaking her bones like a small, wild bird.

"Are you taking me back to Paris?" she asks.

I shake my head.

"Then where?"

She may not realize it, but there's trust in her voice. Like pebbles at the bottom of a lake. I can fish them out, start building something strong again. I broke her trust once. After we escaped the prison I tried to hold her in again, to keep her as my own, very safe captive. I'll be more careful this time around. More careful to make her believe she's free.

I'm not my father. I don't want to hold her captive. I want her to be with me of her own free will. It's only that I can't take the risk. What if she decides to walk away?

I can't hold her captive.

I can't let her leave.

The contradiction is tearing me apart.

"A place I bought for you and your sister to stay until I take care of things with Ian Taggart. He's too dangerous for you to deal with, and after tonight, he'll be pissed."

"Pissed," she says, her voice hollow. "My sister—"

"Will be safe in the house. It's your job to make sure she stays put." And in doing so, it means that *she* has to stay put. Yes, that's the secret to keeping Holly. Her sister.

"That means you need the diamonds."

"I don't need the diamonds to pay off Ian Taggart." I have my own money, as well as my own methods of persuasion to make sure he leaves the Frank women alone.

"Well, I don't want them."

"You can use them to decorate your T-shirts. Your yoga pants."

She glances down at her glittering ball gown. "You knew?"

"I know when a woman's wearing a million dollars in diamonds, yes. Though I am curious about your plan with Taggart. Were you planning on stripping naked in the ball?"

She reaches back and tugs on a few silken ties. The elaborate gown slips from her shoulders, revealing a black sheath dress that hugs her slender body. God, she would have caused a riot in this thing. I'm rock hard just looking at her, my bodily response impossible to control.

She tosses the dress aside. "Good lord, that thing was heavy."

"The problem isn't the diamonds. The problem is the coke."

Her arms freeze in midair where she'd been shaking them out. Slowly she puts her hands on her lap. "My sister is recovering from her problem."

"Your sister needs professional help."

"She doesn't want a rehab center."

Frustration flares inside me. "So you're going

to become an addiction counselor, is that it? Anything she needs? What if what she really needs is a dealer?"

"I won't let her slip."

"This is taking things too far."

"She's *family*. You wouldn't understand."

We both freeze, and it takes me a moment to understand the sensation in my chest. Pain. She managed to hurt me, when I didn't think I had emotions left.

For a long time I had no family.

"I'm sorry," she says quickly. "I didn't mean that."

"Yes, you did. And a year ago you would have been right. I didn't know my family. I didn't want to care about anyone. But I've gotten to know them, my brother Liam. His ward, Samantha. My other brother Josh. I would do a lot for them, even die for them, but I can't live for them."

"I'm not doing that. I'm helping London through a hard spot."

"And you won't stop helping until one of you ends up dead."

She glares at me. "That's not your problem."

"Oh yes it is." I grab her and drag her back onto my lap. Without the heavy fabric, the hard, little diamonds between us, it's like holding her naked. The silk does nothing to hide her breasts, her stomach, her hips. Lust turns me into something else, something baser. An animal. It's taking over and winning. "You made it my problem when you fucking ran from me."

She squirms, trying to escape. It only makes me harder. "Let me go."

"You should know that running only makes me chase you. It only makes me pin you down and fuck even harder as punishment. I was going to wait until we got to the house." I palm her breast, not bothering to be gentle. There's nothing gentle about me right now. "You made that impossible."

"It's not my fault."

I rub my thumb over her nipple and feel it harden. "Not your fault that you're so goddamn beautiful my chest hurts from looking at you? Not your fault that I hurt, actually *hurt* with how much I need to be inside you?"

"No," she mouths, her lips round in the moonlight, the word silent.

"*Yes.*" I shove her hand, crude and abrupt, to my pulsing erection. She gasps as she feels it. Large. Imposing. Yeah, it'll probably hurt going in. That doesn't make me flinch the way it does when she cries. I want her to hurt because of me, *only* because of me.

CHAPTER FIVE

HOLLY

H E PUSHES ME down to the floor of the SUV. My knees feel the carpet and beneath that—plastic and metal. An engine that's barreling at seventy miles per hour.

"Now we're going to play a game."

His voice rushes over my back, my neck like a cold caress. Goose bumps rise. What's he going to do to me? No, I already know the answer. There are only a few things a man can do to a woman who's on her hands and knees. Have sex with me. Spank me.

"Are you going to fight me?" he asks.

"I'm wondering that myself," I say, proud that my voice doesn't shake. I'm shaking on the inside. A quivering mess of worry and reluctant arousal.

He grasps the gold dress and rips. The sound of it splits the air in the cabin, and I flinch. It cost a lot to have that dress made and took even more hours for me to sew the diamonds into it. He takes a long strip of the lace and diamonds and wraps it around my wrist—then the other.

In a few deft movements, my hands are tied behind my back.

The time to fight him has passed.

That doesn't stop me from testing the knots, wrenching my arms to get free.

A sharp pain hits my ass, and I whimper.

"Good," he says, his voice grim. "I like a fight. Now, the game."

"I'm not playing."

"I start a sentence and you repeat after me. *Elijah, when I left your apartment, I went...*"

I close my eyes and rest my face against the seat. Cool leather cradles my cheek. "What's the point of this? You're already angry at me."

Another sharp pain on the curve of my ass. "*Elijah, when I left your apartment, I went...*"

I was out of my mind with worry for my sister. Terrified that Elijah wouldn't help her. That he'd take the diamonds she needed to be safe. "Elijah, when I left your apartment, I went to stay with Marisol and her husband. The French couple. I used the same code you did to seek asylum."

He stills behind me. "You did."

"I threw out our credit cards, our IDs. Anything you could use to track us. They gave us a map of other houses we could stay in, a network of safety that took us all the way to Italy. There we stayed with a friend of London's who's a model."

"Hell." He mutters some colorful curse words. "I went back to the church. I thought maybe you had some kind of Stockholm syndrome, maybe you wanted some closure. And I retraced our steps on the escape, including a visit to the sweet old couple."

"Don't be mad at them."

"I didn't realize they were such accomplished liars."

"I'm the one you hate. I'm the one you want to punish."

"Oh yes." There's a smile in his voice. "I'm going to punish you."

Blunt fingers trace the side of my breast where it's pressed against the seat, my lower back that curves into my ass, the line of my sex through the thin silk. It's a coarse invasion, deliberately designed to move faster than he should. It means, *your pleasure doesn't matter.*

My body doesn't care about this message. It finds his touch unbearably erotic, as if he's awoken something, as if I've been hungry for this entire year.

"Elijah," I say, gasping, needing.

A sharp slap. "I haven't given you the prompt yet. Eager girl. You're adorable when you're horny, you know that? Almost impossible to resist, but I'll find a way. I've been waiting too long for this."

I can't help the tilt of my hips, a candid invitation. "Please."

"*Elijah, I left you because...*"

My insides shrink from sharing the truth, from the emotions it would reveal. His hand is firm against my backside, and I jump. "Elijah, I left you because you locked me in."

He leans over me, his lips a breath away from my ear. "Explain."

That wasn't what I meant to say. *I left because my sister needed me. I left because of family.* Those would have been acceptable reasons. They weren't the real reason I walked away. It was because he locked me in. The same way Adam had. Both men thought of me as some kind of pet. Someone to keep and play with and then put away.

"You didn't treat me like an equal. Like a partner." *You didn't love me.* I manage to hold in those final, damning words, but they hang in the air anyway like dew in a dark morning.

"A partner. Someone to face down the Ian Taggarts and the Adam Blacks of the world, is that what you mean? Someone to hold a gun and fight battles?"

"No."

He bites down on my lower lobe. "Someone to struggle when I tie her up?"

A flush creeps up my cheeks. It's perverse, this game. It's wrong. "*No.*"

Cool air wafts over me as he pulls back. I hear the whistle of a belt, the rustle of clothing. Something hot prods my opening, and I know he's about to have sex with me. He holds himself back, there at the entrance, making me clench around nothing.

His voice comes strained. "*Elijah, I won't leave again.*"

My hands fist against my lower back, and I wriggle my ass, shameless and afraid. "I can't say it, Elijah. I can't. I can't."

A growl of frustration is the answer. He thrusts inside me in one smooth motion, and I cry out. He fucks me hard, almost too hard, and I squirm to get away. Of course I'm tied down and surrounded by him, thoroughly contained.

"So fucking pretty in gold and diamonds," he grunts, matching each word to a thrust. "So fucking pretty in a room full of men and women who want to fuck you."

"They didn't—"

He changes the angle of his thrusts, finding a new place inside me, and my words become strangled. "They did. All of them wanted you. Only I have you. Say it."

I shake my head as tears stream down my cheeks.

"Say it. *Elijah, I won't leave again.*"

But I don't say it.

When he comes with a roar, hands gripping my hips, that roar pervades every inch of the SUV. Hotness pulses into my sheath, and the knowledge that he's coming inside me, unprotected, makes me squeeze down hard. I come in sharp, hard bursts, already grieving the coldness I'll find when it's over, the pain that comes without a promise.

The aftershocks still run through me when he unties my hands. I turn over and push myself onto the seat, feeling topsy-turvy. I rub my wrists. The diamonds left little indents in my skin, like a constellation for me to map.

He's quiet as he cleans himself and rights his suit. He rummages through a cabinet and finds a crystal glass and a bottle of amber liquid. He pours a glass and takes a swallow.

He doesn't offer me any. He just studies me through slitted green eyes.

"So," he says on another swig. "You do plan to leave."

It's strange to have a conversation after he was inside me. Strange to see him so far away. The distance across the SUV could be from here to the moon. That's how far away he feels right now. "My only plan right now is to pay off my sister's debts and help her fight the addiction."

CHAPTER SIX

LONDON

MY SISTER'S IN the next car, probably getting great sex.

Meanwhile I'm stuck with a babysitter who has a stone-cold expression.

Liam North sits across from me in the back of the SUV, occasionally scanning the outside scenery as if we're going through a war zone instead of the beautiful Italian countryside.

The only upside to this situation is that he definitely qualifies as eye candy. A hard body, broad shoulders, and those gorgeous green eyes. Yeah, he's no hardship to look at.

Unfortunately, my mind is stuck remembering dark gray eyes, almost like silver in the shadows. I'm stuck remembering the feel of strong hands holding me while we danced. Adam Black. What a bastard. I should hate him. I *do* hate him.

"Are you sure my sister's safe with your brother?" I ask.

Green eyes study me. He says nothing.

"It's just that he seemed kinda pissed off. He won't hurt her, will he?"

"No."

"Are you sure about that?"

Nothing.

Addiction is not a desire or a pull. It's a third person sitting in the cab of the SUV. It's a physical presence, a shudder, a cold breeze where there shouldn't be.

I turn a ring around my pinky finger, around and around. "The thing is, from what I understand, you haven't known him that long. You only recently reconnected. So he might be the kind of guy to take his anger out on a woman."

"He's not."

"Violence runs in families. Does yours have a history of that?"

He gives a short laugh. "You could say that."

The dark shadow of addiction gives me a little wave, and I resolutely ignore it. "I know I'm being insistent, but it's my sister we're talking about here. I love her. She takes care of me. I wish I could take care of her, too."

It's hard to tell in the shadows but it's possible his green eyes soften. "We'll reach our destination in an hour and a half. You can ascertain her safety then."

"Ascertain," I say, drawing out the word. "Ascertain. It sounds so formal."

"Determine. Verify."

"Still formal. Are you always this uptight, or is it because you're on a kidnapping mission?"

"We weren't kidnapping you. We rescued you."

"Oh, and I suppose if we had wanted to wander back into the party, have another glass of champagne, dance a little, that would have been just fine with Elijah."

Nothing.

"For what it's worth, I think you're always this uptight."

"We're operating in a gray area," he admits. "Private security frequently operates in a gray area. Stalkers we subdue to protect the client. A thief we escort into the police station."

"Not this gray, though. This is like dark, dark gray." Like Adam's eyes. Like the hulking mass of shadows that represents every dark impulse that threatens to destroy me.

"Yes, but in the same way that you want to protect your sister, I want to protect my brother. Even if the danger is coming from himself and his infatuation with—"

I huff a laugh. "Infatuation? Is that what they're calling it these days?"

"What would you call it?"

"Lust. He wants to fuck her." I use the word deliberately, but of course an ex-military man doesn't even flinch at the word. "And once he's had his fill, he'll leave."

"Maybe."

"Definitely."

"What about you? Do you have an infatuation?"

"I'm in love."

It's startling to hear those words from a man so thoroughly masculine and hard lined. I would have expected him to spit nails and break a crowbar in half before ever admitting them. "Let me guess. Your high school sweetheart. You have two point five kids and a minivan."

"Not exactly."

I glance out the window where rows of orange trees pass like flipping through cards in a deck. "Well, we have one and a half hours until we reach our destination," I say, mimicking his low voice. "Plenty of time for you to tell me how it is."

"She was my ward. My daughter, according to the state. It didn't matter that I wasn't her biological father. I swore that I would protect her at any cost."

That makes me lean forward. "This got interesting."

"I noticed her before she turned eighteen." A hard laugh. "To my shame. And then she turned eighteen and noticed me back. I fought the pull but it was inevitable."

"And Elijah has met this girl?"

He nods. "He's been working for my company while he looked for Holly. He's a great agent when he's not distracted by a woman. A real asset to the company."

"That's not my relationship with Holl. We're not an asset-to-company kind of family."

His lips curve in a half smile. "I won't make any claims about us being a healthy family that people should emulate. Most of the time, we're just getting by. You hit the nail on the head about having a history of violence. But Elijah won't ever hurt Holly. You have my word."

"How can you promise something like that?"

"It's a pact we have. All three of us agreed to it. If any of us turn into our father, the other ones will put him down. Like a rabid dog."

A chill runs over my skin, and I curl my legs onto the seat. Possibly this talking thing wasn't such a good idea. *Like a rabid dog.* No, their family is nothing like ours.

It makes me wonder how Holly relates to Elijah. They come from different worlds.

Then again, if it's only sex, they don't need to relate.

Maybe Elijah isn't the only one who needs to get it out of his system. Maybe Holly does, too. The fact is, she'd looked very relieved to see him. This might have started as a kidnapping mission, but Holly had also wanted to be kidnapped.

CHAPTER SEVEN

HOLLY

I HAVE VAGUE memories of falling asleep. My head bumped against the interior of the SUV as we bounced along mountain roads until someone pulled me against his chest. Those same arms lifted me in the night air, and I glimpsed a thousand tiny stars in a black sky. I smelled lemons as he laid me down on something soft. And then I drifted away.

When I wake up, it feels like an eternity has passed.

Sunlight casts a serene glow on the white sheets. I stretch and feel more rested than I have in months. In more than a year, actually. I haven't gotten a sleep like this since I was in my loft in Manhattan. Before I flew to Paris. Before I was kidnapped by Adam.

I'm wearing a thin white shift that I don't recognize. Nor do I remember changing last night. That means Elijah must have changed me while I was naked. A blush heats my cheeks. The only reason he would do that is so I would be more comfortable. It would be easy to push him away if he were an asshole all the time. These small moments of kindness make it harder.

Pink and white marble is cool on the soles of my feet. I cross the large chamber to a set of balcony doors and open them. An expanse of sea bleeds into the sky. The view steals my breath. It's so beautiful and wide. Endless.

Only when I look directly down do I see the cliff and its colorful assortment of houses. We must be high on the Amalfi coast. What are we doing here?

London still won't tell me how she disabled the security system when we escaped. Which means she had help. Probably dangerous help. I'm not sure we'll get that kind of help again. This place doesn't need locks. It has an entire mountain to keep me contained.

A teak dresser has an assortment of clothes. A woman's clothes. I would suspect someone lived in this room, but all these clothes appear new. Some still have the tags. They're all fine quality, with the creases that come from sitting on a store shelf.

They're all perfectly matched to my size, and

they're all… pretty.

I select a white tank top with eyelet lace trim and coral-colored shorts.

Next door I find a similar room with my sister sound asleep in the large bed. She's wearing a similar nightgown to mine, and I have the dark thought that Elijah may have changed her, too.

I tuck the blankets higher on her body against the sea's breeze.

Then I search through the large hallways and rooms until I hear male voices.

"You'll take a team," one man's saying, this voice less familiar.

"I do this alone," says someone I immediately recognize as Elijah. The timbre of his voice searches my body for deep-seated memories. *Oh yes,* I remember him saying, *I'm going to punish you.* My ass still aches from where he spanked me.

The argument abruptly ceases, and I know I've been detected.

I'm still standing three feet from the room, far out of sight of the doorway. My feet were silent on the hard marble floor, but those ex-military instincts have been honed well.

I enter the room and face the man who did unspeakable things to me last night. And his brother. There's a third man in the room I don't recognize, but the green eyes give him away. He's the third brother, Joshua North.

Lord. What am I supposed to do facing this much muscle?

"Hi," I say with an awkward little wave. *Great job, Holly.*

Liam gives me a curt nod.

Joshua North says, "Ma'am," in a low voice.

Elijah tosses down the tablet he'd been holding and crosses the room to me. "What are you doing out of bed?" he says in a soft voice tinged with worry.

"I'm here to help. We're setting up a meeting with Ian Taggart, right?"

"You think you're coming with me."

I glance over his shoulder. Liam is the tallest brother. He's also the leanest. He studies something on his phone as if he can't hear us, even though we're a few yards away. Josh is the most overtly handsome of the three brothers, with a devil-may-care attitude I can feel from his stance. He's also pretending he can't hear us.

And then there's Elijah. He has the largest bulk of muscle.

Even in a plain black T-shirt, the lines of his chest and arms are clear. The fabric falls loosely around his abs, but I know from experience the hard ridges that can be found underneath. His body tapers at his hips, but even his thighs have muscles that strain against his worn jeans.

When I met him a year ago in a French prison, he'd been deprived of light, food, and water. He had been strong, even then, but it did not compare to his size now.

He's a warrior, standing between me and my family's safety.

I lift my chin. "I know I'm coming with you."

A light touch on my elbow guides me out of the room. Then we're standing in the hallway, his green eyes locked on mine, his shadow covering me like a warm, safe blanket. It's alluring, the promise of his strength. All that power used to protect my sister.

If I were a wise woman, I'd figure out a way to seduce him so he bent to my will. I only know how to beat my head against the wall of his will, breaking myself more than him.

His lips hover inches away from mine, and I'm startled by the realization that for all we did together last night, we did not kiss. "Fine," he murmurs.

I stare at his lips. They look firm, but they'll feel soft. Warm. They'll feel like coming home. The invitation entices me enough that it takes me a second to understand his meaning. "What?"

"Fine. You can come."

"I don't understand. Is this a trick?"

That earns me a soft chuckle. "You don't believe me."

"Is this a thing where you tell me we're going tomorrow, but then you secretly slip a sleeping draught in my wine and sneak out tonight for the meeting?"

"No, but that's a great idea."

"The imagination that helps me write books? A blessing. And a curse."

He grins. "I knew you'd come with me, sweetheart. I knew it last night in the SUV when I was spanking that pretty heart-shaped ass. For one simple reason. You know what it is?"

"Because you trust me and know that I can handle this?"

"Because I'm not letting you out of my sight. I trust my brothers, but you slipped my hold once before. I'm keeping you near me so I can make sure you don't bolt."

Tension sweeps over my skin. "And if I did try to bolt?"

An inch, and then his lips nudge mine. It's such a soft kiss, a gentle kiss. Completely at odds with the words that come out of his mouth. "I'd catch you."

Surety radiates from his voice. He would catch me.

The same way he caught me this time.

Why does that bring me so much comfort?

Why don't I want a normal relationship? Regular people go out on dates together. Maybe they buy a potted plant to see if they can keep it alive. Next, a puppy.

That's the kind of partnership I *should* want.

Instead, I crave this man's unholy possession of me.

He has no rights to my body, but he's taking them. Even now he's holding my hips, pressing me close to his, where I can feel his erection. It's almost as if he can't keep his hands off me, and the realization gives me a primal sort of power.

"Get a room," comes the singsong voice of my sister.

I jerk back, guilty, as if I was caught making out as a teenager, but that only rams me into the wall. There's nowhere to go from Elijah's firm hold, and he lets me go with reluctance.

London stands there in a pink handkerchief dress with her hair in a messy knot. There are a thousand tutorials online about lighting and photography for influencers like her, about touchups and Photoshop. But the truth is she always looks like she stepped off the pages of some glossy magazine, the perfect picture of beautiful in a casual way.

She puts a hand on her hip. "Seriously, there are like a thousand rooms in this place."

"Are you hungry?" I ask, feeling anxious already.

That earns me an eye roll. When she speaks, it's to Elijah. "She's always trying to feed me, as if I might be hungry for food instead of hurting for another hit of coke."

"Okay, definitely time for breakfast," I say brightly.

"I'll show you to the kitchen," Elijah says, his gold-green eyes bright with curiosity. It's clear he's planning to listen to whatever London has to say, and the thing is, she's a talker. I cringe internally thinking about the embarrassing secrets she could spill—my strange fixation on Bill Nye the Science Guy in elementary school or my disaster of a prom night.

I'm expecting something utilitarian to match the room upstairs where the men had been meeting. Something with a table and chairs and the basic appliances.

What I find is a gorgeous Italian kitchen with

hand-painted pottery and an older woman covered in flour. She calls to us in rapid Italian, gesturing with her slender arms.

I've picked up plenty while living here, but this is too fast for me to follow.

Without skipping a beat, Elijah answers her in Italian. He gestures to a rustic blue table. "She says to sit down. The bread's fresh out of the oven."

As we sit she starts bringing the food, and it's an entire feast. Fresh bread with a thick crust with soft butter. A platter with sliced meats, cheeses, and grapes. A bowl of panzanella with fresh herbs. Glasses of sweet lemonade are poured for each of us.

"It started in third grade," London says as she piles a thick slab of bread with olives, capers, and slices of salmon. "When I broke my leg."

"London," I say.

"Holland." She uses my full name when I'm being overbearing.

She points her butter knife at Elijah and continues. "So, in third grade. Holl and I were riding our bikes home from school. She was two years older, and better than me at everything."

"That's not true," I say, but of course she ignores me.

"She was biking along, speeding up down this incline, and I wanted to keep up with her. I shouted at her to wait, but she didn't. I think that's why she feels so guilty."

"Guilt is a normal response to the situation." I knew London was slower than me. I knew she was less sturdy on a bike, but I'd gone faster instead of slower.

"Keep going," Elijah says, fixated on what London's saying.

"So I fell off the bike. Broke my wrist and my leg. Our parents freaked out. Everything was tense in the house. And that would have been bad enough, but then—"

"You don't need to do this," I say, but I'm the one who needs her to stop. It's her confession, but it hurts me to hear. It hurts me to hear how she's still suffering.

CHAPTER EIGHT

ELIJAH

HOLLY IS SHRINKING. That's the only word for what's happening to her. She's still sitting there in front of a plate of food that she hasn't touched, but she takes up less and less space with every word out of London's mouth. Part of me wants to shout for London to stop, but I think I need to hear what's going to happen next.

"But then," London continues around a mouthful of olives and bread. "I started taking these pain meds. It hurt really bad, so they gave me the good stuff, which was probably a mistake. Because I took everything that they prescribed, and then I started raiding our parents' medicine cabinet. I didn't even care if it was for pain anymore. Xanax or citalopram. Anything that could change the way I felt, I took it."

"Stop," Holly says, but her sister doesn't stop.

"I started using my allowance to buy shit from our friends' parents' medicine cabinets. And then

I used Holly's allowance. I think that's probably how she found out."

"This is old news. So old," Holly says. "I don't know why it matters anymore."

"You know why it matters. That's when you started covering for me. Eventually my parents found out and they got me therapy, and I got off the drugs. But it never really went away, that yearning. It comes back again and again, like a shadow that I can't shake."

A tear runs down Holly's cheek. "Yes. Okay. *Yes.* It's my fault."

London glares at her. "And that's the problem. It was never your fault. Not that I fell down, not that I got addicted. And definitely not that I developed a cocaine habit."

Holly's face crumples. "Yes, it is."

It looks like London wants to argue, so I murmur, "Enough."

London gives me a significant glance, as if she expects me to fix this. I have no idea how, but I'm grateful that she shared it with me, so I give her a firm nod. It's helpful to understand why Holly is so bent on protecting her sister at any cost. She blames herself.

London stomps her way upstairs.

The housekeeper Emina hums from the garden outside.

We're alone in the small kitchen, and I apply myself to an omelet to give Holly some time to compose herself. After a few minutes she starts to tear a small croissant into a hundred pieces. She opens her mouth. Closes it. Opens it again. "This house," she says.

"This house."

"I saw the locks. The security system."

"We're safe if that's what you're asking." It's not what she's asking.

She glances toward where Emina walked out, without having to enter any secret codes. "I can leave anytime I want?"

"You can." The thought of her walking out makes my chest hurt. "I would come after you, but I won't stop you from leaving. I'm not making the same mistake again."

Her breath catches. "I hope you don't think—"

"You hope I don't think what?"

The words come in a rush. "I hope you don't think that's why I'm doing this. What London said about the bicycle accident and the problems she had after."

"Isn't it?"

"It's not because I feel guilty about London. I know she's an adult. I know the addiction is an illness, not something I caused by riding my bike too fast when I was a kid."

"I'm glad you know that. Because it's the truth."

"Like, yes. It messed me up as a kid, but I'm grown up now."

I study her downcast eyes, the way the lashes brush her cheeks. I could study her for months, for years and not unpack every inch of her. The stories that London shares are my breadcrumbs, but there are no easy answers for a woman as complicated as this.

"That's who your book was about."

She looks alarmed. "What?"

"The book about the tooth fairy. It was about your sister. She's the one in the human world while you didn't belong. She's the one who died."

For a moment she looks stricken. Then she picks up a hard-boiled egg and flings it at me. It bounces off my shirt and rolls to the ground, harmless. "Stop trying to psychoanalyze me."

"Fine," I say, but I know I'm right. That's how she was able to tap into the feelings of grief and guilt so well. That's how she mourned the pain she caused her sister.

"Why are you agreeing with me so much?" she asks, suspicious.

"That's my new strategy. I'm going to agree with you."

"You're a jerk."

"Yep."

"And conceited and cocky and I don't even know what else."

"I could not agree more."

Then she laughs, her head thrown back, the sound like water to parched earth. And I realize I'm officially screwed. I don't just want her body in my possession. I want her heart and her soul. I want every morning with her in a comfortable kitchen where she throws a hard-boiled egg at me. But I'm cursed by family history as much as she is. I don't know how to receive love any more than I know how to give it. It's a hard truth that only those raised in abusive households understand, the certainty that love can only end in pain.

CHAPTER NINE

ELIJAH

LIAM SETS DOWN a cut crystal glass in front of me. Water, the same as he has. The same as Josh. All of us want to have our minds clear for the meeting tonight.

"Now, let's go over the plan," Liam says.

"We did that already," Josh says. "Let's talk about the women in our custody."

I take a sip without looking at him. "Keep your hands off Holly."

Liam pulls up a chair and sits, looking stern and in command even in a metal cafe chair. Josh is sitting in the chair backwards, nice and casual. He acts like he doesn't scan the perimeter every two seconds. Both of their stances match their personalities, one who gives orders, the other who loves to laugh.

I'm not sure what my stance says about me except that I can hardly take my eyes off Holly. I'm not sure anyone could blame me, not with how she looks in that goddamn swimsuit. I'm jealous of a few feet of fabric that cups her breasts, her ass. Even the slight curve of her stomach looks unbearably sensual to me. I want to taste every goddamn inch of her. She's standing waist-deep while her sister swims deeper, and I can feel the pull of her worry from here.

"So the sister is fair game," Josh continues. "That's what you're saying?"

"No one is fair game," Liam says.

"Then why does he get the older one? That's the whole reason we let them come down to the sea, right? Because she smiled and gave him those eyes, and he's pussy whipped."

Hell. "We let them come down to the sea because it could not be more safe with us a few feet away from them. You think one of these tourists is going to best us?"

And because there's a chance it could be the last day on this earth. I don't say that part, but they understand. It's why a soldier goes fucking crazy on shore leave, partying and drinking and fucking. Because it might be the last time.

If this is my last day on earth, I want to see Holly splash around in the Mediterranean Sea. I get to see her bend over as she picks up a shell. And I get to punch Josh in the arm, because he's looking a little too close.

"The sister," he protests. "I was looking at the sister."

London is undeniably gorgeous, like a model who walked off the runway. And she captures a lot of attention in her string bikini and platinum blonde hair. More attention than is really safe considering we're supposed to be blending in.

But for me she doesn't hold a candle to Holly's lush figure and deep, deep eyes.

"Tonight," I say. "It's me and Holly."

"Fuck Taggart." That's Josh.

"Holly thinks I'm doing this because I respect her and trust her and want her to be an equal partner." She doesn't know that Taggart made it a condition of meeting, that she had to be there for us to make a deal. "And hell, maybe it's true. I let her swim in the sea. I bring her to the meeting. I'm turning over a new leaf."

Josh snorts his disbelief.

Liam doesn't take his eyes off the road behind us. He's probably got a nice little catalogue of every car, make and model, that's come by. Maybe license plates, too. It's hard to believe that he ever unwinds, unless you've seen him with Samantha.

"She was worried about Holly," he says.

"London. On the drive last night."

Guilt eats at my stomach. No, I haven't really turned over a new leaf. Not the way I beat her ass last night. The skin became pink, and that turned me on. "I spanked her."

The three words contain a confession much deeper than some kinky sex…

Am I like my father?

How far can I go before I become him?

Have I already crossed that line?

"Did she like it?" Josh asks, and I punch him again. "What? It's fucking relevant."

"He's right," Liam says, softer. "It's relevant."

"She was wet, if that's what you're asking. She came around my dick. I could make her beg for it again tonight, if I wanted to, but that's not the goddamn question."

"You're not like him."

"You don't even fucking know him," I say, louder than I meant. A honeymooning couple from the next table glance over, and I look away. Shit. I'm losing my composure. Not a good sign as I get ready to walk into a deadly situation.

Liam tenses. "You've never told us. What was it like after we left?"

It was already pure hell when my brothers had been home. Our father had a particular dislike of

Liam. Liked to throw him down a well and make him wait hours or even days to pull him back up. Then when he'd gotten older, he'd started throwing me and Josh in the abandoned well instead. He'd left us to cry, to drink the fetid water and then vomit it again, while Liam was forced to listen from the ground, unable to help in any way.

Then Liam turned eighteen. He enlisted.

And then Josh turned eighteen. He enlisted.

It was just me and the old man for four years before I could do the same.

"We don't need to talk about this," I say.

Josh runs a hand over his face. "We really don't. What is this, some kind of intervention? A family reunion? We don't know how to do the hard shit, so why bother trying?"

"It's the reason he doesn't trust us," Liam says to Josh, his voice low, his gaze a rich emerald like our father's. "He knows our secrets by now, but we don't know his."

"There are no secrets," I lie. "You think the old man suddenly grew two heads after you left? No, he was the same bastard he was before that."

Josh nods, looking relieved and exasperated. "That's true. He didn't magically change."

Liam appears unimpressed. "Something happened."

"How do you know?" Josh asks.

"Because there was not a single child services call, not a single police report, not a single record of Elijah at the hospital." My oldest brother leans forward. "So if our father did not magically change into a half-decent parent after we left, how did that happen?"

My throat feels tight. "You don't get to know the answer. You left."

Josh's expression takes on a begrudging approval. "How the hell do you do that? It's like a carnival trick. Instead of telling fortunes, he can ferret out deeply buried secrets."

I look away at the glittering surface of rocks and water. It's a beautiful setting, but all I feel inside is dread. The same thing I feel whenever I think of the past.

Is it too much for that shit to stay buried? Is it too much to want to know my brothers without revealing all the toxic shit? Probably. Yeah, I have a tendency to want too much.

Same thing with Holly. I want her too damn much.

I swallow down the rest of the water and stand. If anyone attacked us right now, I'd be completely dependent on my brothers, because

I'm moving blind and slow.

Underwater in the miasma of memories.

I knew Liam wouldn't let that shit rest forever, but I didn't expect him to bring it up in the wide-open sunlight of the Amalfi coast. That kind of thing deserves nighttime and a dark, scary setting. It deserves blood and gore.

Liam comes to stand on one side of me. Josh on the other.

"Now, let's go over the plan," Liam says again.

"I'm taking Holly."

"I don't understand why we can't come too," Josh says. "A party's a party."

"Because Taggart will bolt. You know that."

"So we pin him down. Put a bullet in his brain."

There's that tug in my chest again. I feel it whenever I look at Holly. I'm looking at her now. "I don't want her to be afraid of me. If I kill him, she will be."

"We're not murderers," Liam says.

That's the problem, of course. He's wrong. I am a murderer. That's one of the secrets I'm keeping from him. It would only pain him if he knew the truth. "Besides, that will make her a target for anyone loyal to Taggart. I want her free and clear of this shit."

"And if something happens to you?" Josh asks.

"I don't give a shit about me. He touches a hair on her head, you burn him to the ground."

I leave them standing on the rocks and stride to the edge of the water. Holly looks up from where she's floating, her hair a mass of curly wet, her eyes sparkling like the sea. She's a siren drawing me away from my ship, toward a violent death. *I don't give a fuck.*

My boots come off with a few kicks, and I'm left in socks and long combat pants. Not exactly the ideal swimwear, but I walk straight into the lapping waves. She meets me with joy in her expression, laughing, and I have a sudden desire to throw off the meeting tonight. Let's fuck and fuck and fuck. Let's forget about the rest of the world in the Mediterranean Sea.

She throws her arms around me. "Hello, Mr. Serious."

That makes me grin. "Mr. Serious?"

"That's your superpower. Being serious."

"You've met Liam, and you think I'm the serious one."

"Well, superpowers run in the family," she says in a reasonable tone.

God, I love this woman. The words come to me in a swell of affection, and I have to turn away quickly to hide my shock. I don't love her. I *can't* love her. That means this terrifying obsession will never end. It means we'll be forever locked in a grid of resentment.

"What were you three talking about?" she says, gesturing to my brothers.

"The plan for tonight," I manage, my voice gruff.

"You got them to agree that it should just be the two of us?"

"I wasn't exactly giving them a choice."

"That was a lot of talking for such a simple conversation."

"Logistics," I say, which is a lie. We went over that already in the house. We'll go over it again before tonight. The truth is we were talking about all the ways I would horrify her if she really knew me.

He knows our secrets by now, but we don't know his.

"Logistics," I say again. "That's all. Now onto the more important questions. We're walking into a dangerous situation tonight, Ms. Frank. Do you know how to shoot?"

"A gun?"

"No, a basketball. Of course a gun."

She shivers, and I see the memory of last night

in her eyes. "No."

"The logistics are pretty easy. Point and shoot. The question is, can you kill a man?"

CHAPTER TEN

HOLLY

WE MAKE THE climb up a winding staircase with crumbly stone steps and a wobbly metal railing. None of that scares me as much as what's coming next. London goes upstairs for a nap. I have no idea how she can rest with what's happening tonight. The other men disappear to make plans. Then it's only me and Elijah behind the house, where a large lemon orchard suffuses the air with a sweet citrus.

Elijah pulls a gun from a harness built into his cargo pants, and I shiver as I realize he'd been armed the whole time we were on the beach. Without any fanfare or warning, he aims at a lemon high in a tree. *Pop.* I jump at the sound. Yellow rind and juice explode.

"We cleared out the orchard and the rental houses fifty yards out," he explains, though I'm reading his lips more than hearing him because of the blast. "It's safe."

Safe feels like a relative term when he hands me the weapon. The gun feels larger than it looked in his hand and heavier than I expected. It's a dark silvery color, warm from where he held it. "Shouldn't there be a safety presentation first? Or a debriefing? Something before me actually shooting this?"

He points to a lemon hanging low. "Go for that one."

"Is there something easier to start with?"

"I'll help you." He puts his arms around me, clasps his hand around my hand. We point at the lemon together. He shows me the sight, and where to aim, but I back away from him.

"Nuh-uh. I'm not ready."

"Like I said, the mechanics are simple. Point and shoot. The hard part is the mindset."

I'm holding the gun like it's a snake coiled to bite me. "What's the mindset?"

"That you need to be ready to kill. You pick up a gun because you can shoot a man."

"Or what if my aim gets good enough where I can shoot a tree branch that falls on his head, and that way he doesn't have to die, and I don't have to kill him."

In a smooth motion Elijah comes to stand in front of me. He holds the gun steady so that it's pointing right at his chest. Even as I yank and pull, it stays right there. I'm afraid to pull any harder or the trigger might go off.

"Go ahead," he says. "Prove that you can do it. Pull the trigger."

"Are you insane? Stop it."

His green eyes glitter in the sunlight. "You can do it, Holly."

"No, I can't. I don't want to." My voice is going supersonic. "You're scaring me."

"Now I bet you wished you'd gone for that lemon."

"How can you laugh at a time like this?"

He grins. "The safety's on."

I'm shaking so hard even when I drop the gun and step back. I could throw up. All over this beautiful green grass. I could throw up all over this orchard. "I hate you."

"You failed the test, by the way. Never pick up a gun unless you're ready to kill."

"I'm not going to kill just anybody. I'd kill someone attacking us."

"Would you?"

I pause, because I'm not sure. Maybe I would freeze, the same way I did with Elijah. Maybe I would go supersonic instead of saving us. Then I remember those cold nights in the French prison.

I'm stronger than I give myself credit for. I'm a survivor. "Yes. I can."

Green eyes study me. Elijah gives a nod that feels like a benediction. "Good."

"I still hate you for that."

A slight curve to his lips. He glances down my body in a way that feels overtly sexual. "We're alone out here. Probably the last time we will be before tonight."

"I hope you're not suggesting we do…" My cheeks heat. "*That.* I'm furious at you."

"I'm not suggesting, sweetheart. I'm telling you to get on your knees."

My body reacts to his command with embarrassing swiftness, becoming wet and warm, readying itself for him. I have to forcibly lock my knees to make sure I don't obey him. "No."

He glances toward the trees. "I'll give you a head start."

"A *what*? We're not racing."

"Of course we're not." That slow grin makes my heartbeat pound. "I'm chasing you. In about five seconds, that is. One Mississippi. Two Mississippi."

"This is ridiculous. I'm not doing this."

"Three Mississippi." He draws out the words, making them slower than they should be.

In that moment I know he's serious.

He's going to make me get on my knees, and the worst part is, the truly humiliating part, is that I would love to serve him that way. The thought terrifies me. I'm supposed to be a strong and powerful woman. At the very least, not on my knees.

I bolt through the trees, heading vaguely in the direction of the house. All the lemon trees look the same, so I don't know if I'm getting closer. I give it every ounce of strength, bounding over uneven ground and stray roots.

"Four mississippi," comes the call from behind me, and I speed up.

I'm going fast enough to hear the wind whistle past me, fast enough that I can't hear when he finally says, "Five mississippi." It's not a sound, it's a feeling. A certainty that my time is up. I dart to the left through the trees, an instinct telling me he's close—and slam right into a hard chest.

The impact sends me flying, and he turns us mid-air, making it so we land with him on the bottom. I collide with his hard abs with an *oomph*, and then tumble across the soft grass.

"On your knees, sweetheart."

It's like I'm in a trance, some ancient obedient that knows I lost the chase, that I've been caught, that I deserve whatever forfeit he demands. I pull up to my knees and wait for him to approach me. He walks over like some conquering Visigoth, and me a conquered village woman. His hand curves against my cheek in a mimicry of tenderness. The cruel set of his mouth proves otherwise. His thumb taps my lips.

"You're going to open and take me all the way down, aren't you? Going to suck my cock like a champ, work my cock until you get your reward. Is that right?"

The crude words make me shiver, and I shake my head. *No.*

"We could do this the hard way, if you want. I might enjoy that. You think I need your permission to fuck your mouth? I don't. I could lay you flat on the ground, kneel on top of you and fuck these pretty lips like they're a pussy."

A fork in the road. One way is the safe direction, the path where I tell him he's disgusting, where I tell him to go fuck himself. The other way is more hazy, more dangerous. It's where I admit the truth, both to him and to myself, the way his words make me wet.

"You can't make me." It's a challenge.

A slow smile spreads across his handsome face. "You think I can't? I'd hold your nose until you had to open your mouth." He puts his thumb at the junction of my lips. "I'd hold your mouth open so you couldn't bite me. And the worst part is… well, you already know the worst part."

Some impulse has me asking, "What?"

"You'd be humping my boot by the end of it, wouldn't you? Desperate to come?"

"Yes," I whisper like it's a confession. Like we're in the dark instead of the sunshine.

"Thank fuck," he whispers back, and it's a break from the part he's playing, a fervent prayer that makes me feel strong. He's the one dominating me, but I'm the one with the power.

He pushes me back until I'm lying on the grass. I know the grass is soft from when I just took a tumble, but the perverse part of me wants it rocky like the beach. I want to feel the sting of his lust, and he obliges by kneeling with his legs on either side of my shoulders. It immobilizes me fully. I can only wriggle my legs, but I can't even lift my arms. I won't be able to control the depth of him in my mouth, the speed. I'm completely at his mercy, and my body responds by turning hot and liquid between his knees.

There's no foreplay, only his zipper cutting through the pleasant air, the heavy weight of his erection against my cheek. He nudges my mouth with a cock already leaking at the tip. "Open for me. Give me that sweet mouth or I'll make you regret it."

I open my mouth, and he immediately invades me—his crown against my tongue, his masculine scent in my lungs, his green eyes in my sights.

"That's right," he says. "You like it, don't you?"

He plunges deep, and I focus on not gagging. My head jerks back, but I'm on the ground with nowhere to go. He pulls back, and I only have enough time to suck in a breath, to register the salt slick of him, before he plunges in again.

His green eyes are slitted above me. "Such a good little whore."

"What the fuck is going on here?"

The words pierce my lust haze, and I struggle to look up. From my position I see an upside-down Liam North staring down at us.

Almost as soon as I feel the pressure, it's gone. Lifted. Elijah stands and pulls me up behind him in one smooth motion. I hear a zipper, and I know he's covered himself. I cover my mouth with my hand, feeling a rush of humiliation to be caught in this position. It feels like I'm a teenager caught with my boyfriend in the basement.

Adrenaline pumps through my heart. I have to remind myself that I'm a grown-up who can do dirty things with other grown-ups.

"What did it look like?" Elijah asks, his voice challenging.

"It looked like you were holding her down and fucking her mouth."

"Then that's what I was doing."

My embarrassment morphs into something more nervous. There's a strange tension shimmering in the citrus-scented air, a conflict I don't fully understand.

From around Elijah's arm I can see Liam's expression, the usually stoic man now forbidding and outraged. "You don't get to talk to her that way."

"Then stop me," Elijah says, a rare hollowness in his tone.

I force my way past him. "Hey, wait a second. This is embarrassing and everything, but what we were doing wasn't illegal or even wrong. It was two consenting adults."

Liam doesn't take his eyes off his younger brother. "It didn't look like consent."

Shock holds me immobile for a moment as I process this. Liam thinks his brother was forcing me to do something. He thinks his brother was using me, violating me.

That's why he interrupted us. That's why he's challenging his brother.

So why didn't Elijah just tell him that I wanted it?

Then stop me.

"It was consensual." I stamp my foot, which feels childish but the two men are posturing like fighting bulls and ignoring me completely. "It *was*, okay? I wanted it like that."

Liam finally focuses on me, those green eyes intense with emotion, and I suppress a shiver in order to stand up for Elijah. "You wanted him to hold you down and speak to you with disrespect? You wanted him to call you a whore?"

There's no judgment in his voice, but there is a thread of disbelief. I can understand that. I'm having a hard time understanding my desires, too. Did it spring from the shadows of that French prison? Do I only like this because I was captured? Or was it already part of my being, only awakened when I met Elijah?

The lemon orchard has no answers. "Yes," I say.

Liam's voice turns soft. "Are you saying this because you're afraid of him? I can protect you."

That decides me. If I had any doubt, it's vanished, because I'm not afraid of Elijah. Confused, enchanted, turned on. He inspires a myriad of feelings in me, but not fear.

"No," I say, my cheeks flaming under the sun. Without the storm of desire surrounding me, what we did feels sordid. "I'm not afraid of him."

Liam studies me. He studies his brother. What does he see? A man made of the same flesh and blood? Or a monster? Finally he gives a curt nod and walks off through the trees.

I turn to Elijah, who's staring at some place in the blue sky, his expression hard-set. "That was... that was crazy, right?" I say with an awkward little laugh.

He doesn't laugh or smile. He doesn't even meet my eyes. "We should get back to the house."

"Elijah?"

He stalks away, following his brother without answering me.

CHAPTER ELEVEN

ELIJAH

A LITTLE MARKET at the base of the mountain sells dimpled grapefruit and homemade pasta and hand-painted pottery. That's where we leave Liam and Josh. My concession to doing this with Holly is that they're nearby with an open radio connection.

I drive up the narrow road, my eyes on the trees, wondering how many men Taggart has stationed. One of them pretends to change a tire in his beat-up truck. Another one watches from the porch of a small shack, rocking on a chair with a black cat in his lap. No doubt Taggart knows our precise progress up the mountain to his mansion.

Holly sits in the passenger seat, silently shredding a napkin she found in the center console. The floorboard is covered in white confetti. I know she feels bad about what happened this afternoon. I should say something reassuring, but

I don't feel reassuring. I feel pissed off. I'm angry that Liam broke things up, that he assumed the worst, even while I'm wondering if it was right. Maybe I am becoming my father. Where is the fucking line? I should tell Holly that I care about her, that I'm sorry about earlier, but what I really want to do is tell her to finish the blowjob she started while we drive to this meeting.

"We should talk about what happened," she says finally.

"Should we?"

"Yes." A firm answer that's belied by her nervousness. When she runs out of napkin, she picks up the pieces on her lap and tears them into even smaller pieces. "We should."

"I don't know what there is to say. My brother caught us fucking."

"And you thought you were taking advantage of me."

"Wasn't I?"

"No."

"Right," I say, a hollow feeling in my chest. "Other girls want roses and dates at nice restaurants. You like to be fucked after I teach you to shoot a gun."

"Well," she says, her tone reasonable. "I didn't really learn how to shoot the gun. I don't think you should count on being an instructor or anything. It's not really your strong suit."

Humor licks at the dark cloud that's been hanging over me, and I have to fight the quirk of my lips. How does this woman manage to make me laugh when I'm ready to pound a concrete block into dust? "What should my profession be, then?"

"I mean you're very good at this whole fighting soldier thing, but I guess... I guess you don't do that anymore? Your work for the government? The whole undercover thing?"

"I was honorably discharged." In other words, they were forced to release me because I had way too much dirt on the higher-ups. In particular, the lieutenant colonel. It was either let me go peacefully or order a hit. Part of me still looks over my shoulder for an assassin.

"So now you work for your brother?"

The hollow feeling is back. "Sure. Unless he fires me."

"For having sex?"

"For forcing you to have sex. For degrading you. For using you."

"You're not giving me any control over the situation."

I know I'm being an asshole, but I can't help

the taunting tone. "I thought that's what you like, isn't it? Me taking the control from you? That turns you on."

She looks away, and I feel about two feet tall. What a bastard. Maybe I should knock her around for a few hours. Maybe then I'd really feel like my old man.

"Look," I say, keeping my voice even. "Liam may not have been right about what he saw in that orchard, but he was right about one thing. I'm not good for you."

"You're wrong. You've already saved my life more than once. And now look, you're coming with me on a dangerous meeting so I don't have to go alone."

"Did it occur to you that I like the danger? That it's my exit strategy?"

"Your exit strategy? What do you mean?" And then my meaning sinks in, and her eyes widen. "Don't say that, Elijah North. Don't you dare say that."

I turn my focus back to the winding road, but it doesn't matter. I can say it or not. The truth is I've always had a death wish. As long as I can remember, I've been waiting for the killing blow.

Pink stucco rises from the cliffs, and I know we've reached our destination. Satellite maps already confirmed that Taggart's compound is large and well fortified. We're basically walking into a lion's den. We only walk out if they let us.

If it was only me, I wouldn't give a shit. That death wish comes in handy.

But it's not only me. Holly is here, and I need her to be safe like I need to breathe.

"Let me do the talking, okay?" I say as we pull up to a wrought iron gate.

It's a sign of how nervous she is that she doesn't immediately argue.

Men with semi-automatic weapons approach the car.

We're escorted into the mansion, up the marble steps and through a set of double doors of carved wood. The mosaic on the entrance features a large black dog and the words *cave canem,* a nod to the same flooring at Pompeii.

Sure enough, the sound of barking greets us as we step into an open-air foyer.

I'm not particularly worried about the dogs. I assume they're like the men holding semiautomatic weapons—they only attack on their master's orders.

Two large black pit bulls round the corner, and Holly makes a sound of surprise.

Concern strikes my chest, because if Holly

acts afraid, if she *runs* from the dogs, they might chase. Because I'm a bastard who wants her to suck my cock, I've never asked her the things I should know. *What's your favorite color? Are you allergic to any food?*

Are you terrified of dogs?

I move to stand in front of her, but she brushes past me and gets on her knees. One of the dogs pauses, clearly taken aback by this show of trust. The other one wags its tail and runs up for a belly rub. The more cautious one follows behind, its bark more hesitant.

Okay, I guess she loves dogs. And she makes even snarling beasts into pets.

Ian Taggart enters the room and snaps his fingers, and the dogs immediately jump up and run to him. It makes me think he let them in on purpose to scare us. That worked, because my heart is still pumping double time out of fear for Holly. I thought she might get her throat torn out right in front of me. Instead she made kissy sounds.

She looks at the dogs with longing, clearly wanting to pet them more, but then she straightens. "Taggart. We have business to conclude."

He smiles. "I was wondering if you would insist on coming."

She pulls out a velvet pouch, and the two men with weapons start forward. Ian Taggart waves them back. He holds out his hand, and she places the diamonds in his hand. "It's all there. More than she owes you. And in return you are to leave her alone."

"As I told you, I'm not the only one she owes."

"That will be my problem, not yours."

"And it's hardly going to matter if she's still addicted to blow. There's always another dealer ready to give her a supply on credit."

"Again, that's my problem."

"You have a lot of problems." He smiles. "I could solve a few of them for you."

"Not interested."

"Because you have a problem solver of your own," Taggart says, nodding towards me.

"I'm not here to solve her problems," I say. "She's doing that by herself. I'm here to blow your brains out if you touch a hair on her head."

"You have a reputation," he says, unmoved by my threats. "If you're looking for work…"

"I'm not."

He gives a reluctant nod. "Then I agree to your terms."

I take Holly by the hand in case she gets any

cute ideas about petting the dogs again before we go. I really wouldn't put it past her. "There's just one more thing," Taggart says, and I pause.

"Yes?"

"That Interpol agent. Who is he to you?"

He was my mentor at the beginning. Now we're enemies. Rivals.

Because he became a traitor. Or was that me who betrayed him? Neither of us has pure intentions. Especially when it comes to Holly Frank.

"He's no one," I say before leading Holly out of the lion's den.

"One more thing," Taggart says, clearly amused. "You may have been worried about coming here, but you worried about the wrong thing. I like Holly. That's why I didn't bother turning her in for the bounty a certain lieutenant colonel has placed on her head."

CHAPTER TWELVE

LONDON

"I SHOULD HAVE been there."

Holly ignores me and continues chopping onions. Tears are dripping down her face, but she's determined to help in the kitchen. I'm pretty sure Emina gave her this job on purpose.

"I'm serious," I say, awash in both fear and gratitude. "You should have told me you were meeting Ian Taggart. And you should have taken me with you."

"Does it matter?" she says. "Everything worked out."

"How would you have felt if Elijah went and didn't tell you?"

Guilt flashes through her dark eyes. "It's not the same. You're not well."

That's what she says about me. *You're not well.* It's what she says instead of saying, *you want to blow cocaine until you're so far out of your mind you'd fuck anyone, do anything.* That's what she says instead of saying, *you're a fuckup.*

I grab an onion and start chopping. I have no idea how many onions we need, but if she's going to help cook dinner, then so am I. I've always been like this, the follower, the copycat. People look at us and think it's the other way around, but I've never understood why. She clearly has her shit together. She's smart and calm and collected. I'm a mess.

"I'm healthy," I say, my voice flat. "I'm just hooked on coke."

"Addiction is a sickness."

The onions are getting to me, too. Tears trickle down my cheeks. "Is it? Because it doesn't feel like a sickness. It feels like a weakness."

Actually, it feels like a person.

He's standing behind us, a shadow that only I can see. He alternately cajoles and threatens me, but in this battle of wills, he's winning. If there were a line of cocaine in front of me, I would sniff it. It would be his hand on the back of my head, forcing me down.

"You're not weak," Holly says, basically sobbing as she sniffles and cries. It's probably not safe for her to be wielding a butcher knife. "You're strong. So strong. I wish you could see yourself the way I see you."

"If I were strong, you wouldn't have needed to protect me from the meeting with Taggart."

"Ugh, there was no reason for you to see him again! Not after he took advantage of you."

I finish chopping the last half of an onion, and Emina sweeps in with a bowl to gather the chopped onions. Then a large platter of tomatoes appears in front of us. I have no idea whether this is some kind of therapy technique where we talk out our feelings using vegetables as a medium. Or if Emina is just using us to get her prep work done faster. Maybe both.

Holly and I both reach for a tomato.

"So, it's over now. I'm safe. We're both safe."

"Of course," she says, chopping off the green top. "It was completely uneventful. He took the diamonds and promised to leave you alone."

Something about the way she says *of course* makes me think she's lying. That she's trying to protect me again. "You mean he promised not to loan me any more money."

"Tomato, tom-ah-to," she says, shoving aside the chopped pieces and grabbing another tomato.

Tomatoes are a lot harder to chop than onions, I discover. They don't make me cry, but they're so ripe and juicy that they melt under the knife instead of slicing into cubes. "It could have been dangerous. What if he decided to get violent?"

"That's why I took Elijah with me."

I snort. "As if he would have let you go alone."

"You want to talk about overprotective. He's the overprotective one. I didn't even need to shoot a gun. And for that matter, he didn't actually give me one."

"A gun?" I set down the knife. "What are you talking about, a gun?"

She looks guilty. "He may have taught me how to use one. Yesterday. After we came back from the beach. But if it makes you feel better, he's a terrible teacher."

"That makes me feel worse, thanks."

"Look." She pushes aside another pile of tomato cubes and faces me. Her voice drops to a near whisper. "That wasn't the scary part. The scary part was when Elijah and I... we were... you know I mean... well, we got busy."

Despite my annoyance at my sister, I can't help but laugh. "You got busy?"

"Very busy."

"And that was... scary?"

"The scary part was when Liam caught us. He got really pissed off."

"What? Why?"

"I guess he thought Elijah was forcing me or something. The tension was off the charts."

A chill runs over my skin. "Liam told me something when we left the costume party." I need to do something with my hands, so I grab a tomato and begin chopping. "He said the three brothers have a pact. They all agreed to it."

"What kind of pact?"

"If any of them turn into their father, the other ones will put him down. Like a rabid dog."

"*What?*"

"And I'm guessing forcing a woman would be like his father."

"So Liam was threatening to *kill* Elijah? His own brother?"

"I guess he feels like he'd be doing the right thing. Like doing it for his own good. Apparently their father was a real piece of work."

"But Elijah wasn't even defending himself. He didn't even explain that I liked it or that he basically asked permission first, and it was all consensual."

I feel my eyes go wide. "Um, what exactly were you doing with Elijah that needed explanation? I thought you were talking about getting busy."

"Like I said, we were… very busy."

"Euphemisms don't really work for this. Why did Liam think you might be forced?"

"It's possible that I was on the ground being held down by Elijah. It's also possible that a certain part of him was in my mouth and he was calling me names."

"Oh my God." My cheeks turn hot. "Holly!"

She grabs a tomato and begins chopping. "I know."

That's the kind of thing people would expect from me, but I've never been held down by a man *like that*. And I never would have guessed that Holly did things like that.

Emina bustles between us, gathering the chopped tomatoes into a large bowl. She sets down a platter of zucchini for us to chop next. She says something in rapid Italian. And then in heavily accented English she explains, "Men are never satisfied. They want to hurt us and they don't want to hurt us. They want to please us and they don't want to please us."

She disappears as rapidly as she came, pulling something from the oven and humming off-key.

Holly and I exchange glances. "Men," I say.

"Well," she says. "I'm not sure about *never* satisfied, but Elijah was particularly not-satisfied because Liam interrupted before he could... you know."

My cheeks heat, but I can't help but tease her. "Say it."

"No!"

"So you can give a blowjob but you can't say it."

"Stop!" She looks scandalized. "You don't think there's something wrong with me, do you?"

"God, no. Sis. Don't worry about it. As long as you were having a good time, that's what matters. The brothers will have to sort out their shit between themselves."

CHAPTER THIRTEEN

LIAM

"**H**IT ME AGAIN."

I throw a punch, one that Elijah could block if he wanted to. He doesn't want to. It slams into his jaw and sends him staggering back. When he rights himself blood drips from his lip. "Goddamn," I say, throwing in a few extra curses. "If you want a fucking beating, find a dive bar."

Elijah wipes his face with his forearm. "Don't pretend you didn't enjoy it."

A battered picnic table holds a few bottles of water and towels. They're the only equipment we need for a solid workout. That, and each other. Josh and I are already covered in sweat from our sparring. Elijah joined us, but he's busy fucking around.

I take a swig of water. "If your goal is to prove I'm like our father, fuck you."

"Hell," Elijah says, taking off his shirt. He's clearly just getting started. "I thought you might want to blow off some steam. Especially after what happened in the orchard."

Josh perks up. "What happened in the orchard?"

"Nothing," I growl.

Elijah smirks. "Your brother caught me in a sensitive position."

"So?"

"So, he thought I was forcing Holly to suck my cock."

Josh was lying down on the grass, taking a breather after our last round. He sits up now and whistles. "What the fuck? And neither of you bothered to tell me?"

"I'm telling you now." Elijah points at me. "Now fucking fight."

"Not if you're just going to stand there and let me beat you. Fight back."

He grins. "I thought you'd never ask."

This time, when I throw a punch, he blocks it and spins around, aiming for my kidneys—a serious shot. I manage to twist but take the impact to my stomach. I jump back to catch my breath, hands up in case he attacks. "I thought you were forcing her because you had her pinned to the ground. And because you called her a whore."

"Kinky," Josh says.

"Kinky is handcuffs and a safe word. Not what I saw."

"You shouldn't have seen anything." Elijah throws a roundhouse kick, and I block it, but I'm less prepared for his followup sweep. I jump, and retaliate with a one-two punch that lands on his shoulder. He strikes with a backhand. "It was a private fucking moment."

"Next time close a door, then. Don't fuck out in the open if you want privacy."

"The point is that you don't have to assume the worst."

I run a hand over my face, dropping my guard for a second. "I'm sorry."

Elijah snarls. "I don't want an apology. I want to know why you thought I was like our father. You think I slap her around, too? You think I throw her into a goddamn well and make her beg for fresh water? You think I laugh when she drinks the rotten sewage and then vomits?"

We only have a few rules to our sparring sessions. No grabbing, no biting. I slam myself into him, my shoulder to his stomach, and he grunts in pain. We tumble to the ground, and I pin him down with my weight alone. "You want to know the truth? I think you're walking a fine fucking line. And I think you like it that way. Maybe you wanted me to see you in that orchard. Maybe you want me to put a gun to your head and pull the trigger."

With a hard twist, Elijah flips back onto his feet and slams me down on my stomach. I spring up before he can pin me down. He has more strength, but I'm more agile. And both of us have stamina to make this a fight to the death.

Josh shoulders his way between us. Both of us back up. It's never happened before. We practice daily to stay sharp. No one's ever had to break up a fight.

I'm breathing hard. Elijah is, too. Only vaguely I'm aware of the ache on my shoulder and my side from where he nailed me. He coughs, probably because I blasted him in the stomach.

Josh points at Elijah. "You. If you want a bullet in the brain, then fucking do it. Don't make Liam do your dirty work for you." Then he points at me. "And you. The worst part wasn't our father telling us we had the devil inside. The worst part is that you believed him."

My throat feels tight, and I stalk away and stalk right back. "I don't believe him."

"Part of you does. The same part that made you fight your attraction to Samantha."

I make a sound of possession. "I fought my

attraction to Samantha because she was my ward. I was supposed to take care of her, not lust after her."

Josh rolls his eyes, which makes me want to rush him, too. "We have more important things to do than fight each other. For example, what about the lieutenant colonel?"

Suspicion makes my eyes narrow. "What about him?"

"Apparently he's in the country."

Elijah sighs and grabs a towel. "Apparently there's a bounty on Holly's head."

"Fuck."

"I know."

"There's only so far we can go to protect her if he tries to use his position."

Elijah narrows his eyes. "I'm not letting him take her."

"I'm not suggesting we let him take her, either. I'm suggesting we tread carefully here. The last thing we need is an international incident." The fact is fighting the lieutenant colonel is extremely uncertain territory. The wrong move could be an act of war. I've seen too much bad shit working in the shadow ops to have much country loyalty left, but that's going far, even for me. My business is back in the States. The love of my life is back in the States.

"Tread carefully," Elijah says, his voice flat.

I love my brother. I would sacrifice anything for him, including my own life.

But I won't sacrifice Samantha Brooks—not her safety or financial security or even her ability to travel internationally to perform the violin.

I glance at Josh because I need his help with this. He's a little bit closer to Elijah as the middle brother. And he's a natural peacemaker, whereas I'm a controlling bastard.

"Tread carefully," Josh says, his tone easy. "As in we cover our tracks."

Elijah gives a curt nod. "I'll confront him. And there won't be any link back to you."

I shake my head. "That's not the point. You confront him, and you come back alive. Otherwise I'll have to explain to Holly that you got beat by a middle-aged man with a fake tan."

That makes him snort, which is a good thing. We're back on neutral territory. "Got it."

"And take Josh with you."

Elijah raises an eyebrow. "You really think he's going to best me?"

"I think the man is wily and untrustworthy and corrupt in the extreme. There's no telling what lengths he'll go to in order to get what he wants."

"Have we actually discussed why he wants Holly?" Josh asks.

"Because she's the key to controlling Elijah."

"I don't know why he thinks that," Elijah mutters. "Or why he wants me so badly. I'm just a soldier. He has plenty of those."

"You're one of the best," I admit. "In-fucking-valuable."

Josh nods. "And anyone with eyes can see that you're head over heels for Ms. Holland Frank. That makes her a target, while you're busy getting kinky."

"All right," Elijah says, gesturing toward the clearing where we sparred. "Your turn."

The thing about Josh is that he's a trash talker. "Liam may be too pussy to beat your ass, but I'm not. Step up, little brother. Let's get this party started."

I settle back on the bench to watch the match.

Josh has a deceptively languid fighting style. It looks as if he's only half paying attention, as if he's barely even trying, but he can drop someone twice his weight that way.

Elijah has a more direct fighting style, but damn if it isn't effective. The ache in my shoulder can attest to that. Not many men can get a direct hit in with me.

This lieutenant colonel is going to be a problem.

Elijah may not understand it, but I do. There are plenty of soldiers out there. It's harder to find someone smart who can think on his feet. Someone strategic. Someone with the brains to back up the brawn. He had the best soldier in his arsenal, and he wants him back.

The question is how far he'll go to get him.

Using Holly as a pawn is a risk.

That implies a certain level of desperation. And desperation is danger in a man like that. Elijah will confront the lieutenant colonel, but I doubt that will be the end of it. Josh will provide backup and make sure Elijah doesn't strangle the man.

The last thing we need is to be the subject of an international manhunt.

CHAPTER FOURTEEN

ELIJAH

I'M IN THE shower when I hear someone behind me.

Steam clouds the glass, but I recognize the figure on the other side. Short stature, a wild mane of honey-colored hair. In some ways she looks ordinary. That doesn't explain the instant pounding in my chest. The anticipation in my hard cock.

I open the door, revealing my naked body, the water streaming down. Her brown eyes are hungry as she takes me in. And then shocked.

"You're hurt."

I give a short laugh. "This is nothing."

She reaches into the spray, touching her forefinger to the corner of my mouth. "It's not nothing. You're bleeding. Did Liam do this to you?"

"I asked him to."

She shakes her head, not quite understanding.

That's fine, because I don't understand it either. I only know that I wanted Liam to do it. I wanted him to punish me for walking too damn close to the line. What I did to Holly was wrong, depraved. He was right to stop me.

"What are we going to do about the bounty on my head?"

"I'm going to see the lieutenant colonel."

"You're trying to protect me again."

"The same way you do for London."

That makes her smile, though it's a sad one. "Do you think it's kindness that makes us want to protect people? Or is it arrogance, thinking we can handle what they can't?"

"I don't know." I put my head against her forehead. "You're the one who's good with words. The only thing I know is that I'm made for pain."

"Made for pain?" She brushes a hand against the bruise on my stomach.

"Let me take your pain, sweetheart." *It's the only thing I can give you.* I don't have it in me to love her, to promise some long-term commitment.

I don't have anything to give her but the shelter of my body.

I expect her to reject the offer, to insist that she's strong enough to carry her own pain. It's a sign of how tired she must be, how scared, that she nods, her gaze never leaving mine.

She reaches for the hem of her shirt, and my blood pumps faster. Then it's off her body, revealing the gentle bounce of her breasts. She goes to her skirt next, pushing down the white flowy fabric. She's a feast for my eyes. Narrow waist, wide hips. Shapely legs.

And the beautiful thatch of brown hair at her core that calls to me.

She steps inside, and water droplets land on her breasts, her stomach. They catch on her eyelashes. Her hand reaches for me, but I turn her around. I want this to last, and if she touches me, I'll spurt against her smooth body in a matter of minutes.

I cradle her head in my hands, and the trust she gives me is immediate, reclining back, letting me move her under the hot spray until her hair is soaked through. I should probably have something fancy in here with rosemary and lemon, instead of this plain shampoo. I pour a generous amount on my palm and smooth it across her hair, a dark brown now that it's wet. Then I work my hands into the thick locks, gentle so I don't pull, thorough so the foam works through. She moans as my hands work over her scalp, and I spend more time massaging her.

Then I rinse her hair, slowly, carefully, until it looks like silk again.

When I turn her back around, her lids are low. "You're beautiful," I tell her, which feels inadequate. I don't know the right words for this ache in my chest. Beautiful only means her face and her body. Beauty means what's on the surface, when it's her whole self that radiates with comfort, with love. With a sense that I've found home.

Her lips curve in a small, sensual smile. This is the confident Holly. The one who never worries if men prefer her sister, the one who ignores the critics and the naysayers. This one knows her power. She's fully herself. And I'm almost dropped to my knees in awe.

The baser instincts win out.

My cock aches with the urge to be inside her. Warm velvet. Slick friction.

She drops to her knees, and the sight of water trailing down her breasts makes me weak. "I want to finish what I started," she says, her eyes a thousand feet deep. A well that I can fall into and never come out. "No interruptions this time."

It's with regret that I remember kneeling over, fucking her pretty face. It's with regret and a deep vein of lust. "You don't have to do that, Holly. You don't have to do anything you don't want to."

"Let me show you what I want," she says, taking my cock in her fist. She's still a little untried despite her bravado, her hand clumsy around my slick cock, uncertain and too gentle. Then she kisses the tip, and my eyes roll back in my head. God, it's good.

"Fuck," I say, unable to stop the words tumbling out of my mouth, the degradation I seem determined to heap upon her. "My cock filling your mouth, your lips stretched around me. That's what I want to see. Take it deeper, sweetheart. Faster now."

Her eyes go wide, but she tries so hard. She tries so hard, and that turns me on even as it makes me want to push her further. How far will I take this game?

When does it cross the line?

My hands come to rest on her head. "Stay still now. Let me fuck your face."

She pauses, clearly uncertain. Then she nods.

"Good girl," I say, my voice hoarse, and I'm already thrusting inside. Already pushing my cock into the warm well of her mouth, already lost to the insanity of desire.

I bump against the back of her throat, and she gags.

Fuck, but the sound of that turns me on. A normal man shouldn't want to debase a woman he cares about. A normal man doesn't need to get inside her throat more than he needs to breathe.

"I'm gonna go deep, okay? You can take it, can't you?"

She doesn't quite answer this time, but I push inside anyway. Past the pressure fighting me, past the entrance of her throat, until she's gripping me like a sweet vise.

I hold there for one second, two, three, while tears leak down her cheeks.

When I pull out she gasps, sucking in air around my cock.

"You're such a good girl. Such a brave girl," I tell her, petting her hair. "I know it's scary when I put my cock all the way down your throat, but you're so strong for me."

She coughs, spraying water against my stomach, and I want more of that. I want her gagging and choking on my dick. What's wrong with me that I want that?

So I drag her to standing and lean her against the wall. She's still panting, her chest rising and falling with heavy breaths as I kneel between her legs. I want her broken for me in every single way. I want her wet and sloppy and clenching hard because I made her come. I want the taste of her pussy ingrained so deep in my mind I remember it even when I'm asleep.

I hook one of her legs over my shoulder and rest her weight on me, so she won't fall. Then I lean into her sex. That's the only word for it. I lean. I press my face against her damp curls. I breathe in deep that beautiful feminine musk.

When I finally lick her pussy, I moan at the flavor. A few laps at her clit, and she's rocking her hips, trying to get more contact, humping my face. Every kind of debasement turns me on, including this one. She begs me with her whimpers and her cries.

Seconds from coming, on the edge of the abyss.

I pull away.

She keens a sound that makes my dick twitch. *Perfect.* She's perfect.

"Don't stop," she pants, but I have this perverse desire to make this last forever, as if I can stave off tomorrow with pure sex. No danger, no separation, nothing but this.

I shut off the water, and the room becomes suddenly silent without the rush of the shower.

There's only the sound of our breathing and the faint droplets of water that fall from our skin. I lead her into the bedroom, one that's similar to hers but on the third floor. Directly above her, in fact. I've stroked my cock in this bed, imagining her below me.

We're still wet, still slick when I toss her onto the bed. She half gasps at the coldness of the air, half laughs as she rolls away. I grab her ankle to catch her but the water makes me lose my grip, and she squirms away. So I tackle her with my whole body, using my weight to catch her against the mattress, to subdue her. Her smile fades, and she looks up at me.

Her hand touches my lip again, and I become aware of the throbbing. I hadn't even felt the pain when I'd been fucking her pussy with my tongue.

A notch forms between her eyes. "Why would your brothers hurt you?"

"It was nothing. We were practicing sparring. I should have blocked it."

"You blame yourself?"

"Maybe I wanted to feel pain." To feel something, anything.

Confusion mars her pretty face. She doesn't understand.

Of course she doesn't. For all the ways that we

are alike, for all the beautiful darkness inside her, she had a good childhood. She feels things deeply—love, concern, even betrayal. It's why she rebels so hard against the control I try to place on her.

I find myself telling her things I've never told another living being, even as my cock nudges against her opening. There are two kinds of intimacy happening right now. "When Liam left, Josh and I stayed there. When Josh left, they assume I stayed there, too."

Her brown eyes widen. "You didn't?"

I push myself all the way inside her sweet pussy, and the clench almost kills me. It's what makes it possible for me to continue. It's like she's connected into the place deep inside me, the one with all the secrets and all the fear. "Good old Dad liked to kick us around, but when Josh left, he went a little crazy. He just kept going, without anyone to stop him, and I thought…" I pull out and fuck back into her cunt. "I thought he was going to kill me that night."

She bucks her hips, trying to dislodge me, trying to stop the sex. It feels wrong, talking about my shitshow of a family while I fuck her. I know it feels wrong, but that's why it works for me. My wires are all crossed inside. Maybe one too many blows to the head.

"Didn't even make it to the hospital. Just dragged myself to the woods behind our house. Slept there for a couple nights until I could make myself stand, and I left."

Tears are streaming down her face, and it makes me hard. It makes me hard just like when I fucked her face and choked her little throat. "Elijah."

"I lived on the street until I was old enough to enlist." The memories have sharp teeth and claws. They threaten to rip out my throat so I can't speak. My next words come out hoarse. "The things I did, Holly. You would be disgusted with me if you knew."

"I wouldn't." She pushes against my chest, and it shouldn't move me. There is not nearly enough muscle on her slender frame to dislodge me, but it works anyway. I roll over onto the bed, and then she's on top of me, my cock still in her cunt. "There is nothing you could say—"

"Don't," I say, too sharp. "You have no fucking idea."

"Maybe not," she says, her hips moving, rocking. She's riding me. "Maybe I don't understand what you went through, but I do know my feelings. I know you can't change them."

Her pussy clenches around my cock, and I grunt in pleasure. "I got numb on the street. So fucking numb that I thought I wouldn't be able to feel anything. Only pain could make me feel anything at all. Until you. You make me feel other things, terrifying things, but, Holly... God, Holly, what terrifies me is that sometimes even you aren't enough."

Determination darkens her eyes. I didn't mean to lay down a challenge, but that's the way she's taking it. She puts her palms on my chest and lifts up, bearing down fast enough to make me catch my breath. Then she's fucking me, riding me, a beautiful blur, and I throw my head back, unable to do anything but take it. My hands clench her thighs, and I know there will be ten finger-shaped bruises there tomorrow. Is that the line? Where is the line? Then she comes, her pussy drenched with arousal, her secret muscles clenching me, and I don't care about the fucking line. I thrust up into her, hard, coming in hard, wrenching, painful spurts.

She collapses onto my chest. I gently push her onto her side, away from me. There are only inches between us, but they might as well be miles.

I can't believe I told her about my time on the

streets. I may not have embellished with the details, but she's a smart woman. She can figure some of it out.

Fuck. I've never told anyone that, and for damn good reason.

It's me at my lowest point. Desperation. Hunger.

And endless, endless pain.

"Elijah," she whispers. "Let me come with you."

I stare at the ceiling when I answer, my heart a cold stone in my chest. "That's the difference between London and me. She needs you. I don't, sweetheart. You can't help me. It will be easier on my own."

CHAPTER FIFTEEN

ELIJAH

THE MEETING IS set for noon. We leave with exactly enough time to get there. Normally we'd arrive early and scout the place, but the lieutenant colonel will expect that. There will likely be traps and a few rifles pointed at our heads. Anything we do to protect ourselves can be seen as an act of war against the American government. So we're going with only a couple of knives and a handgun. Barely anything by our usual standards. It's a risky move, but not going is not an option. The lieutenant colonel won't shoot me on sight. If he only wanted me dead, there were easier ways to accomplish that. At least I'll hear what he has to say before I tell him to go to hell.

"So," Josh says. "You and this writer chick. You're an item?"

Over the past year I've gotten to know my brothers fairly well. Liam is the serious one, the upstanding one. He would not interfere or even ask about my personal life—except if he thought it was a safety issue. On the other hand, Josh is more casual. He's comfortable throwing out a question like that without any preliminaries.

"Don't get me wrong," he continues, kicking his boots up on the dash of the black SUV. "I'm not judging you. It's more of a congratulations. She's hot in a sexy librarian kind of way."

I don't say anything. I also don't punch him in the face and crash the SUV into the Mediterranean Sea. So I'd say that I'm winning right now.

"That being said, I still don't understand why you don't get a little sister action going. The other one's hot in a Cosmo cover model kind of way, and if you could get both of them into bed—"

"Is there a point to this?"

He grins. "I knew I could get you to talk."

Out of the three brothers, I'm the most taciturn. "You want to talk about relationships? Do you also want to braid each other's hair?"

"Listen, I know we were basically raised like feral wolf cubs, but this is a normal thing. Brothers talking about a girl they're interested in while we go on a road trip."

"A road trip? We're going to confront a rogue military officer."

He grins. "So it's a good road trip."

The road curves sharply, and I deftly steer to avoid sliding off the mountain. The road down the Amalfi coast is precarious, and even worse, one lane for much of the way. That means we get stuck behind a string of sputtering old Volvos and tour buses with no way to speed up.

The cars in front of us roll to a stop, and I'm guessing there was a fender bender ahead. "So if you want to talk about a girl you're interested in, how about you go first?"

"A girl? A single girl?" He snorts. "I'm interested in lots of girls. No one in particular."

"That's not what Liam said when he got drunk that one time."

Josh straightens. "When was that?"

"When Samantha left." Liam was her guardian until she turned eighteen. Then she turned the tables by approaching him. Sexually. He was unable to move past his guilt at taking advantage of her and she walked away from him.

"God, he was a fucking disaster during that time."

"Imagine if she hadn't taken him back. We'd be stuck with that asshole."

In addition to excess drinking and a complete lack of sleeping, he trained until he literally dropped from exhaustion. It was dangerous and depressing.

"What did he say?" Josh tries to keep his voice light, but I can tell he's affected.

"Something about a girl you met a few years earlier. What did she do? Some kind of dancing. A burlesque dancer. Or maybe a stripper. Did you date a stripper?"

He speaks between gritted teeth. "She was a ballet dancer."

"Oh, that's right." I smirk. "I knew I could get you to talk."

The cars ahead of us begin to move again, and we pass by a truck driver arguing with the owner of a Toyota, both of them gesturing. They found a small turnoff by an abandoned gas station to have their disagreement.

"Fair's fair," he says, his tone still artificially light. "There was a girl. A ballerina. We had a fling. Her brother threatened to kill me. I plotted his demise. It was all very Shakespearean."

"Have you actually read Shakespeare?"

He snorts. "She didn't enjoy being used as a pawn by the US government."

"God, none of us do."

"She also blamed me for most of it. Which I deserved."

"So she left your sorry ass."

"Saw right through me. Somehow you've managed to fool a sexy librarian into thinking you're worth a damn. She's not even mad about being a pawn for the US government."

"She will be if I don't get this goddamn bounty lifted." The bounty on her head is not an official order from the US government, of course. Like most of the things the lieutenant colonel does, it's off the books. Plausibly deniable. Shadow operations.

"So does this lieutenant colonel want to fuck your ass or what?"

"Hell if I know. It's a control thing with him." At least he agreed to a meeting. Of course he did. How else could he make his demands? "He wants to own me."

"And here I thought that was Liam's job."

My hands tighten on the steering wheel. "Was she the one?"

"You think that's a real thing? Soul mates and all that shit?"

"I don't know. Liam and Samantha seem pretty real."

"The thing that gets me about soul mates is, if we all have them, then even evil bastards have them. Maybe our mom was really our dad's soulmate. Maybe she was destined to be beaten and bruised because of some goddamn scroll written in time."

I glance at him sideways. "Have you been smoking pot this morning?"

"I'm just saying. Soul mates aren't only for the good people."

"So you're saying assholes like us have a chance?"

He snorts. "You might. As long as you don't fuck it up with Holly Frank."

I swallow around the knot in my throat. It's hard to believe in hope when you've held on to despair for so long. It's hard to imagine a happily ever after when all you've ever known is pain. Maybe my brother is right.

Maybe soul mates aren't only for good people.

Maybe bastards like me get one, too.

CHAPTER SIXTEEN

HOLLY

*T*HE FISHERMAN WORKED *the nets for three long, hard decades. He heard the old wives' tales about sirens and monsters, but he only believed in what he could catch. His face grew lined with the whipping of the wind. His knuckles turned into hard knots. And every sunrise found him on his boat.*

One day he felt a hard yank on the nets, and he pulled them in. A large weight fought him, bigger than any fish he'd ever caught, and he worried about a dolphin with its fin trapped.

It took every ounce of muscle in his seasoned body, but when he finally pulled the haul onto the deck, it was not a fish or a dolphin. It was a woman. More specifically, a mermaid.

He approached her with the wonder of a child, but she was panicked, thrashing, tears in her large blue eyes. "Shhh," he told her. "I won't hurt you. Let me help."

His large hands were deft as he cut into the knots

and freed her.

"What's your name?" he asked, but she crawled to the edge of the boat and threw herself into the water, disappearing in a flash of silver-purple scales.

The next day he went back to the same place and waited, no net in the water. For hours the sun beat down on a dry, empty deck and endless water. When he despaired of finding her again, he saw the same flash of silver and purple. She swam right up to the boat and put her hands on the helm. This time she had no fear, not of his muscles or his knife.

He approached her cautiously. "What's your name?" he asked again.

She gave him a mischievous smile and swam away.

On the third day he did not wait for her to arrive. When he reached the same spot, he anchored the boat and stripped down to his briefs. Then he dove into the water. He swam in large, arching circles—a search pattern—trying to see into the deep waters.

She was underneath him, watching, curious and delighted with this human she had caught. He was hers. She didn't tell the other mermaids about him, because she didn't want to share.

Only when he began to tire did she swim up to greet him, thumping his legs with her tail and flicking her hair over her shoulder. He laughed, the sound rusty from disuse.

Weeks passed. Months.

He began to wonder if he loved her, and if she could love him back. Most days the mermaid would come play with him. On some days she would not, and he began to grow resentful of whatever business kept her away those times.

In his small crofter's hut, he began to build a net, the largest one he'd ever made.

When it was finished he hauled it onto his boat and threw it into the water. He caught her. He caught her, and this time, he didn't immediately let her go. In that moment it ceased being a game. That is where the love story ends and the real story begins.

THE KNOCK COMES two hours after Elijah and Josh leave. I've been scribbling in my notebook ever since they left. My new story idea has cramped my hand. It's been a long time since I wrote about mermaids. Not since my first published book. It must be the seaside setting that's inspired me to write about what creatures inhabit it.

I'm only halfway curious when I hear voices downstairs. There are occasional deliveries of food from the local merchants.

Liam appears in the doorway, and I know something is wrong.

His green eyes appear dark, and though it's an expression I've never seen on his face before, he's worried. He gives me a curt nod in greeting. "The lieutenant colonel is here. The man Elijah is supposed to be meeting. I called him, but it'll be another two hours before they make it back."

A sense of surrealness washes over me. I know my blood is pounding, but everything is happening in slow motion. The sun seems brighter, the details on the terrace sharper. Leaves that had only been green are now vibrant. The sound of waves rushes in my ears. "What does he want?"

"He wants to talk to you. I would tell him to go fuck himself… but he has an arrest warrant for you from the AISE. The Agenzia Informazioni e Sicurezza Esterna. We're in their country. They have jurisdiction."

My voice turns into a squeak. "They're going to arrest me?"

There's a telling pause. "No, but it would be hard to stop them. Easier to give in to the lieutenant colonel's demands. He claims that if he talks to you, only talks, he won't make the arrest."

"He wants to talk to me?"

"Most likely he's going to ask you about the

diamonds. That's what he really wants. Well, he wants Elijah, too, but I think at this point he'd settle for the diamonds."

Panic makes my throat tight. "We don't have them anymore."

Liam's green eyes look so much like Elijah's, it makes me ache. "Be honest with him. He would spot a lie anyway. Once he knows that Taggart has the diamonds, he can try going after him. If he has AISE in his pocket, he might even get them back."

"Do I have to do this?" Part of me is terrified to face the man that even makes Elijah blink, despite all his muscles and confidence. The other part of me is curious to know who this man is and what sort of hold he has over the man I've come to love. It's more than just the coercion. There's some strange bond between these two men. It keeps Elijah tethered more than any bounty on my head. Even his brothers haven't managed to break that hold.

Liam shakes his head. "There's a chopper about a thirty-minute drive from here. We can slip out the back with London and be off the ground before they can stop us. But…"

"But we'd be running from the authorities."

"It wouldn't look good."

"Would you get in trouble?"

"I'm more concerned for Elijah. We'd have to leave him here until we could get an extraction team. He can take care of himself, though. And Josh is with him."

"I'll talk to him."

Liam can't entirely hide his relief. "I'll be in the room with you. And we have our security team stationed at the door and outside. He can't hurt you."

I suspect that isn't quite true. This lieutenant colonel has taken on almost mythical proportions. It feels like almost anything is possible, but maybe it's good that I get to talk to him. I might uncover what hold he has on Elijah. I might learn how to break it. "I should talk to him alone. You can wait outside the room."

Liam raises his eyebrows. "Are you sure?"

"No, but I have a feeling he would insist on it even if I didn't."

Liam studies me. After a long moment his lips curve up. "You're good for Elijah," he says, and before I can process that statement or respond, he's gone.

I close the notebook where I'd been writing and set it aside.

Then I stand and pace in the few moments

left that I have alone. The second-floor landing opens to a small balcony. Wrought iron furniture. Ivy on the walls. It's a picturesque setting. The beauty doesn't match the conversation I'm about to have. Because unlike Liam, I don't think the lieutenant colonel will be satisfied with diamonds.

Liam appears at the door again, this time preceding a man of middle age. He's not wearing a military uniform. Instead he's in a black suit, but it's clear from his bearing and his haircut that he's army. His skin has a splotchy redness that makes him look perpetually angry. He smiles, and my skin crawls. I would look away if we passed on the street. Now I force myself to meet his pale, watery eyes. "Lieutenant Colonel Jefferson," I say, holding out my hand.

He grasps my hand with a sweaty palm. "I see my reputation precedes me. Don't tell me that our dear Elijah has been sharing classified information."

The implied threat makes me flush. "Of course not."

He gestures to the small wrought iron table and its two chairs. "Please. Sit. It's such beautiful weather. We can have some lemonade." He gives Liam a significant glance. "Perhaps you can get it for us."

Liam gives me a hard look. "I'll be right out-side the door if you need me."

I nod, even though the taste of fear is metallic in my mouth. I'm in the room with a sociopath. That much is clear to me from even the few words we exchanged. There's something reptilian and flat about his eyes. This is the man who Elijah reported to. This is the man he served.

When we're alone, the lieutenant colonel settles into one of the seats. I'm more slow to occupy the other one, perching on the edge as if I need to bolt.

He gives me a frank assessment. "Pretty, but I don't understand the fascination."

Indignation rises in my chest, but I force it down. I return his assessment with one of my own, taking in his florid face down to his scuffed dress shoes. "Powerful, but not nearly important enough to control Elijah North."

He gives me a tight smile. "I see his kitten has claws."

"You wanted this meeting."

"To see why Elijah walked away from his rank, his career. To be frank, why Elijah North walked away from me. I created him, after all. I can destroy him, too."

"I think if you could do that, you already

would have."

"You think? Then you underestimate how valuable he is to me. It would be like blowing up a shiny new Black Hawk. A complete waste. The military already has more than enough waste. Assets like Elijah North are rare. And important to national security."

"I don't need Elijah to tell me classified information to know you're dirty. So far I've seen you try to steal diamonds, put a bounty on my head, and create a fake arrest warrant. You don't get to talk to me about national security."

"My dear. I forget that you're naive. National security isn't achieved by following the rules. It's not the pretty speeches that politicians give on green lawns."

"So the arrest warrant for me is about national security?"

"I picked Elijah out of nothing." His pale eyes grow even paler as he grows more intense. "He would still be a low-level grunt on some shithole base if I hadn't picked him out—his psych eval, his tests. A personal interview. I found him. I *created* him."

God, no wonder this man isn't going to give up Elijah. "You're insane."

He smiles that reptilian smile again. "I'm

trying to help him."

"Leave him alone."

He glances casually at his watch, an overlarge monstrosity that's probably waterproof and can tell the time in eight different time zones. "At this moment, our good friend Elijah North is being charged by the United States for treason."

Dread pools in my stomach. "You're lying."

"I don't have to lie. You'll find out soon enough."

"This is your fault."

"Contrary to what you may think, I don't control the entirety of the American government. There are things beyond my control. I tried to help Elijah, but he didn't make it easy, traipsing across borders with a civilian in tow. He should have known this would happen. He would have known that if he hadn't been so blinded by lust."

I'm stricken for a moment. Maybe I am the reason that Elijah is in trouble now. If I had never landed in that French prison cell with him... he would still be working for the lieutenant colonel. It would have been a cold existence, but would it have been safer?

Then I look into the man's reptilian eyes, and I know the truth. He would not have been safe with him. He was a tool. A machine that this man deployed on his enemies. Not a living, breathing person. He would only be safe until the lieutenant colonel was done with them.

And he would never have reunited with his brothers.

No, I don't regret meeting Elijah in that French prison. That doesn't mean I'm still good for him. Without me this man holds no leverage over him.

I raise my chin. "What do you want from me?"

"Walk away, Ms. Frank. Go back to New York City."

My throat clenches. "If he follows me?"

"He searched for you because he thought you wouldn't be safe. He has a hero complex, our Elijah." He says those words with such smug possession, as if he's sure of his hold over Elijah. And for all I know, it's justified. Elijah walked away from him, but maybe he only did it to protect me. What happens when I don't need protection anymore? "He's not a man who enjoys domesticity. Watching reruns with a box of takeout? No. He won't follow you."

My chest aches, because I recognize the reality of his words. We've been living in a world of danger and subterfuge. It's been horrible in some ways. In other ways, it's… exciting. I think that Elijah thrives on that excitement. He needs it, much more than he could ever need me.

We are fundamentally different creatures. He's a tiger. I'm a mouse. We played together for a time, but there's no future. I can't last in his world, and he'll never fit into mine.

"What if he doesn't let me leave?" It's strange, the hope that springs out of the words.

"That's why I suggest you leave before he gets back. I can secure transportation, though Liam North can also do that." He glances back toward the empty doorframe. "Couldn't you?"

Liam appears, his expression hard as granite. "Holly, you don't have to listen to him."

Unfortunately I've already heard the truth. I've already seen the future. "Would you help me leave if I wanted to? Take that chopper you offered with my sister?"

"We can wait until Elijah gets back."

He won't let me leave, not until he ascertains my safety. He won't believe that I'm safe, and once he's sure of it, we'll have an awkward goodbye. I glance at the lieutenant colonel. "Will you allow that?"

A shark-like smile. "It would be better if you were away. In fact, if you leave immediately, I can have the arrest order lifted, the bounty removed, and the charges against Elijah dropped."

"Not that you admit to being responsible for any of those things," Liam says, his voice hard.

"No," the lieutenant colonel says with that same smile. "There are too many confidential things to share, but everything I do is for the uniform."

That's a lie. Everything he does is for himself, but that doesn't mean he's wrong in this case.

You can't help me. It will be easier on my own.

He said that to me only last night, and I had felt myself shrivel up even as I lay on the bed, my body still warm from his lovemaking, my heart freezing cold.

"What will you do with Elijah?" I can't help but ask.

"We'll have words, I'm sure," the lieutenant colonel says. "Perhaps he'll come back to work for me. Perhaps he won't. Either way you'll be out of the picture."

London needs you. I don't, sweetheart.

It isn't my place to worry about him. He doesn't want it to be my place.

"Okay," I say in a whisper. And then louder. "Okay."

Liam swears under his breath. "Elijah

wouldn't want this."

He may not want me to leave, but he doesn't want me to stay either. He wants to keep me safe, and I learned last night what a cold companion protection could be. I want more than he'll ever give me. Love. Companionship. I want a partner. "I'm going. The only question is whether you'll help me. I'd much rather take a North Security jet than go with him."

"What a dilemma." The lieutenant colonel looks so pleased with himself. "The infamous Liam North with his impenetrable sense of honor. You can help the woman leave or you can do what your brother would want."

"This is what my brother would want," Liam says, his voice grim. "If she's leaving, she's leaving with me. You won't lay a finger on her."

Gratitude and guilt war in my chest. I don't want to cause a rift between the brothers, especially now that I understand how precarious their relationship is.

"I'll show you out," Liam says.

The lieutenant colonel nods and stands stiffly. Only as he walks to the door do I notice the slight limp. I wonder if he got the wound in combat. He's far too snake-like for me to feel sorry for him, though. He wields his control over Elijah like a weapon.

"One more thing," he says, pausing to look at me. "If Elijah does come find you again, however unlikely, our deal is off, Ms. Frank. You may think I'm cruel, but I understand him better than you ever will. He needs the work I'm offering. You would only strangle the life out of him."

CHAPTER SEVENTEEN

HOLLY

A VINE CURLS up the front porch of the small and stately house, leaves bright green against white paint, the occasional pop of pink. A butterfly dances from flower to flower, brilliant in the sunshine. The house is the setting of every happy memory in my life. Not the times we were traveling. Only here did I ever feel completely safe.

The SUV rolls to a stop on the gravel path. Before we're even completely still, the door flies open. My mother has beautiful blonde hair. She's the very image of my sister, London, who's sitting beside me. Mom pulls at the driver's side door, but it's locked, nothing happens. I'm already pushing out of the backseat, stumbling out of the high step.

My mother grabs me in a bone-crushing hug. "Holly," she says over and over again. "Holly. Holly. Oh my God, Holly. London." I'm released so she can grasp my sister the same way.

The next few hours are a blur of tears and homecoming.

Walking inside feels like stepping into my childhood.

The fridge has none of our childhood artwork or travel photos. Instead there's only a single postcard taped to the stainless steel front. I know without examining closely which one it will be. The one I picked up at a busy tourist stand in Paris and slipped in the mail. *We're safe. We love you.* That's all it said. It was all I could risk telling them at the time.

Despite her shock, or maybe because of it, she insists that Liam North and the other men in our security entourage come inside. She produces a large bowl of chicken salad with grapes and walnuts, focaccia bread, and sliced watermelon.

My father arrives a few minutes later from the automotive store where he'd been. My sister and I are both collected in a hug that smells like rubber and oil.

"Where the hell have you been?" he asks, his voice hoarse with emotion.

I press my face to his barrel chest. "It's a long story, Daddy."

"I've got all year. Did you get into some trouble? Why didn't you call me?"

"I couldn't."

His expression hardens. "I knew it. Someone hurt you. Did someone touch you? I'm going to kill them. I'm going to call the cops. Hell, I can't even decide which one. Who hurt you, sweetheart?"

Hearing him use the word *sweetheart,* the same endearment Elijah uses, makes my cheeks heat. "Don't call the cops. It's complicated."

Complicated doesn't begin to describe the experience of the past year. For example, there may or may not be a warrant out for my arrest in multiple countries. The lieutenant colonel promised it would go away, but exactly how long would that take?

Daddy's expression darkens. "Whatever you two got mixed up in, we can fix it."

I glance at London, who's being hugged by our mother. And probably grilled, the same way I'm being grilled by my dad. London was always the spitting image of our mother. Whereas I take after my dad more, sturdy and strong. We're earthenware while they're teacups.

"I don't know how to tell you," I admit in a whisper.

Liam North appears at my side. He nods to

my father with that military precision he has. "I'd be happy to fill you in, sir, if you'd like."

"Yes." Daddy pulls me into a tight hug. "You're not going to disappear when I turn around, are you, pumpkin? I was worried about you."

"I'll be here," I promise, hot tears welling in my eyes.

He steps outside with Liam North, and London follows them outside. I can still hear the rumbles from inside the kitchen as the other men finish eating.

That leaves my mother and me alone in the living room.

She clasps me close again. "Holly. What on earth? Why aren't we calling the cops?"

"It's a long story," I say, the same thing I told my dad.

The look she gives me is knowing and infinitely patient. "Then let's go sit down in the bedroom. I need a pillow to hold while you tell me this."

I expect her to lead me to my old bedroom upstairs but instead she takes me to the master bedroom. If walking into the house was like stepping into my childhood, climbing onto the California king bed is like reverting to my toddler state. I feel warm and safe. As if a thunderstorm is outside the house, but it can never touch me here on this embroidered bedspread. She hands me a velvety throw pillow, and I wrap my arms around it. Then she sits close, close enough that I can feel her warmth.

Something that had been strong for the past year, competent and cool, that part of me cracks. The comfort of the room is a hairline fracture. The compassion in her touch is what breaks me into a million pieces. I begin to cry, dropping large, hot tears onto the pillow.

"Oh, Mama," I say on a sigh. I haven't called her that in over a decade.

She takes my hand in hers. "You know you can tell me anything."

It's something a lot of parents say, and I know that it's true for my mother. I could tell her about liking a boy or even smoking pot. But this will be pushing the edges of any parent's understanding. It's already pushing the edges of my own.

I take a deep breath. "A year ago, I was kidnapped."

Her hand squeezes mine, and I see her take a deep breath. After a moment her hold relaxes. "The police can be here in a matter of minutes. They can do tests, take evidence—"

"It's… harder than that," I say, unable to meet her eyes. "There was a man in the cell with me. His name is Elijah. He helped me escape. I think… I think I may have fallen in love with him."

Her blue eyes turn glossy with tears. "Oh, baby."

"I know what you're thinking, that it can't be real love in a situation like that."

"There are things I've never told you about my relationship with your father, about the way we met. Maybe I should tell you soon, but for right now I need to hear your story."

"Well, he had enemies. They wanted to use me against him. And he was so determined…" My chest heaves, and for maybe the first time in the transatlantic flight I register that he's really gone. I'm alone now. "So determined to protect me that I felt like maybe he loved me, too. That was just an illusion, though."

"Are you sure about that?" she asks, her voice gentle.

"No," I say with a watery laugh. "I'm not sure of much these days."

"And London? She looks thin."

"She's sick, Mama." The words come out as a whisper. "That's what started this mess. She needed money to pay back debts, because she's… she's addicted to cocaine. I've been trying to help her myself, but it's so much, it's so scary, and I just—"

"Shhh," my mother says, squeezing my hand. "You have help now."

Yes. I have help now. For all that Elijah was determined to protect me, it was a very specific form of help. My own personal bodyguard. But I've needed a different kind of help, and my mother can provide that. "I think she needs rehab."

"We'll worry about that," she says. "Did you think you needed to carry it all on your shoulders? London is my baby. She'll always be my baby. I love that you care for your sister, but she's not your responsibility. You know that, right?"

My brain understands, but my heart rebels. It wants to fix everything and everyone that I love. Including London. Including Elijah. "That's why I left. Because I was a danger to Elijah. As long as I was around, he'd just keep protecting me and protecting me. It was toxic, that form of protection. He didn't even want to let me leave the house."

She hesitates. "Holly, you know how your father and I met?"

"You were on your road trip. You met him at a diner. He bought you dinner."

"Yes," she says, drawing out the word. Her hands fidget, tugging at the embroidered fabric of the bedspread. "The truth is he was… pushy. He was in a bad place, and he did bad things."

I stare at her. "Mama, what are you saying?"

"I never thought I'd share this with you, but—" She gives a small, helpless laugh. "I suppose you definitely are my daughter."

It's strange, the pride I feel at that sentence. London was always like my mother. Always beautiful and delicate and vulnerable. Everywhere we go, people know they're related instantly. I'm the odd daughter. The different one, but I can't mistake the rueful possession in her voice. The certainty that we are alike in some deep, ineffable way.

She looks into the distance, and I know she's seeing the past. "There are things I won't tell you, things you shouldn't know. But your father was in a dark place in his life. He took it out on me. He did things that were… unforgivable." She focuses on me here, in the present. "I forgave him anyway. There are people who would call that weak, but I prefer to think of it as strength."

"Are you saying that I should have stayed with

Elijah?" My heart lifts just thinking about the possibility. It's only been twelve hours, but already I miss him.

"Goodness no. I hardly know anything about this man. Some of that's because we haven't had much time, but I suspect you're leaving a lot out on purpose. No, I don't think you should be with him. I'm saying you should get to make your own decision now that you're grown. And no one, not even your father or I, get to judge you for them."

My throat feels tight. "Thank you, Mama."

"So what happens now? Are you still in some trouble?"

"No, I'm safe now." Even though it had felt gross to negotiate with the lieutenant colonel, there had been some relief at being able to manage the situation. Some power, too. It had felt better than sitting in some ivory tower, waiting for Elijah to rescue me. "I think... I think I'd like to go back to my old life. To feel like my old self again."

The woman who had not needed a man in her life. A career, friends. I'd had everything I needed. There is no space in my life for a man who needs danger to feel alive. Even if it feels like leaving him left a hole in the center of my heart.

She pulls me into a hug, both of us still seated

on the bed. The warmth of her arms, the weight of them, makes my chest hitch. There are moments to be a strong, independent woman. And there are moments when you can fall apart. In my mother's arms, I release every weapon and line of defense. There's only me, missing a boy, loving him from afar, as I sob against her shoulder. She holds me for what feels like hours, murmuring sweet nothings.

CHAPTER EIGHTEEN

HOLLY

I'M WASHING DISHES when my dad comes into the kitchen. He stands next to me, staring out at the deck through the picture window. Mom and London are drinking tea, both of them casually gorgeous. My dad built the white Adirondack chairs himself. Beyond them you can see endless rows of gravel paths and garden beds. It looks like a photograph in a glossy magazine about quaint cottage living.

No one would guess that the younger one was hurting for a line of coke.

"Are you going to tell me what happened?" my father murmurs.

"It's a long story."

"You've been here three weeks."

It's been a restorative three weeks, being pampered by our parents, feeling protected in this place where we spent parts of our childhood. My mother has been very understanding of our secrecy. She agreed to keep the story private, knowing that my father would lose his mind.

My father wants a name and an address. He suspects some of the things that happened, and he wants to commit murder.

"It doesn't matter what happened," I say, my voice light. I'm home now. The thought of him facing off with Elijah makes me shiver. I love them both, and a meeting would probably end with one of them dead. Elijah is a hardened soldier, and my father is tough in his own way.

"How can you say that?" He picks up a dish and begins drying. I know it's his attempt to appear casual when he really wants to bend a crowbar in half. But he already tried stomping around. He already tried yelling and threatening, but we've been silent. "Someone hurt you. That much is clear. There's a sadness about you that wasn't there before."

The sadness is from leaving Elijah. The sadness is from missing him, but telling that to my father won't help. Not if I have to explain that I met Elijah in a prison cell. "Listen. There are people out there who could hurt me. They could hurt *you*, so it's better if I don't say anything."

As soon as the words are out of my mouth, I know they're wrong. He looks furious. "Let them come after me. Do you know what it does to me knowing I failed my little girls? That you needed protection and I wasn't there for you?"

"Dad, I'm all grown up. I have been for a while."

He sets the dish down and pulls me in for a hug. "You'll always be my little girl. And I wanted to be overprotective. Maybe I still was. Your mother stayed my hand, because of the way she was raised. With a fist so clenched she couldn't even breathe. Did she tell you that?"

"No, but she said something about the way you met."

He looks away. "Hell."

In this moment he sounds like Elijah. "I thought she met you on a road trip."

"That's a nice euphemism for how it happened. The same way you keep telling me that you decided to travel the world on the spur of the moment."

I squeeze him back, the strong, protective solidity of him. "There are some things that only make sense to the people who experienced them. You raised two girls who know how to take care of themselves." That much is true. We evaded experienced security professionals. We faced off against international thugs and made it out alive.

"Now you need to trust us."

He kisses my forehead. "You might be right about that. Some things only make sense to the people who experienced them. But I'll tell you this much. You ever point a finger at someone, you ever so much as nod in their direction, I'll rip his fucking throat out."

I give him a watery smile. "I love you, too."

I leave him to the rest of the dishes and go upstairs. I've settled into my old bedroom and London into hers. It's been a safe haven here at home, but it's getting time for me to leave. London has already been accepted into an upscale rehab center only an hour's drive from here, and Elijah is…. In the past.

My cell phone sits with taunting darkness.

Of course he could get my number. He could call me all gruff and angry with me for leaving. Or he could call me acting all casual, as if I only stepped out to the store. I have a faint smile on my face just imagining it. He could call me. But he doesn't.

For three weeks I've maintained radio silence. With shaking hands I pick up my phone and call the number Liam gave me. The words *Liam North* flash on the screen. His private cell phone.

"Hello," he says, sounding brusque and businesslike.

"Hi, it's me," I say. And then with a little laugh. "Holly. Holly Frank."

"Hello, Holly. Is something wrong?"

"Oh no. Nothing like that. I only… wanted to see if Elijah is okay."

There's a pause. "Why are you asking?"

"Well, you know, he did save us from Ian Taggart and help with that. I wouldn't want him to be hurt or anything. You know, hurt physically. I know I can't hurt him emotionally." I'm rambling, and it's only by clamping my hand over my mouth can I stop.

Liam clears his throat. "He's fine. Angry. I have a nice shiner."

I wince imagining Elijah punching his brother. "He didn't mean anything by it. Don't be angry at him. He loves you and Josh so much."

"You don't have to defend him, Holly. I understand why he did it."

"Oh. Well." There's a tightness in my throat. A tingle behind my eyes. I'm near tears just thinking about Elijah. Maybe I need my own rehab center. Not recovery from cocaine. I need to recover from Elijah North. He's the addiction I can't shake.

"Holly." Liam's voice softens. "He's gotten on

with his life. You need to, too."

The tears spill over. "Right," I manage. "You're right."

"He'll be safe this way. And despite what you might think, I don't hate my brother. I want him to be safe from the lieutenant colonel. You did that for him. You saved him."

CHAPTER NINETEEN

HOLLY

'M MISSING A shoe. I hop around my loft apartment with only one high heel on my feet, the other bare and stockinged. I'm wearing a white T-shirt with the words *I read past my bedtime* on it. The black pleated skirt and heels will make it vaguely professional.

"Are you on your way?" comes the voice from my phone. It's sitting on the entrance table on speaker, because I'm supposed to be out the door.

"Very, very soon."

There's a laugh over the phone. "That means no. It's a good thing I made the appointment for thirty minutes after two instead of two o'clock sharp."

I glance at the clock. A smile hovers on my lips. "You knew I'd be late."

"Because I know you," comes the singsong answer. My agent is more than my business partner. She's been my friend since I sent my very first round of queries, and she replied back, "Let's hop on the phone. Right. Freaking Now."

She loved my tooth fairy story, but it hadn't been the first novel we sold. She shopped it to publishers who said it had great writing but was too strange to be accepted by readers. Give them a vampire, please. But I've always had an aversion to blood.

They finally relented when I wrote a shifter story for them. Only when my books cracked the New York Times bestseller list for young adult were they willing to take a chance on the tooth fairy. She's my highest grossing book to date, and the sequel has been a major success.

Finally I spy my shoe hiding underneath a tall bookshelf. I fish it out and slide it on, then I'm out the door. Then back inside again as I've forgotten my laptop bag.

"Coming," I say into the phone, breathless as I press the elevator button.

"Good," she says, her voice tinny. "This mermaid book is going to be big. I can feel it."

"I hope so."

"I'm heading into the elevator. I'll shoot the shit with Trinity for half an hour, then we'll meet you at the cafe down the street for lunch."

"See you soon!"

Despite the number of books I've written, I haven't actually met my editor that many times. There were a few awards ceremonies, a panel at an author convention.

Once, I received an official invitation to visit the publishing house, but from what I could gather, the main purpose was to snap photos for their Instagram account.

They had a sheet cake with my book cover on the top, the castle of teeth artwork even more startling on something meant to be eaten.

The elevator begins to close, but someone slides his hand between the doors.

Only distantly I realize that I don't know the man wearing a hoodie and jeans, who steps onto the car and stands in front of me. I can't see much of him from this angle, but I would remember those broad shoulders if I'd seen them around here. Then again, a lot has changed in a year.

Maybe some of the tenants I knew have left.

Hopefully the guy who plays oboe is one of them.

I'm digging through my purse, looking for some lip gloss to swipe over my lips. It's been so long since I got ready to go out that I've lost the hang of it. But I'm determined to fit into my old life, so when my agent suggested we have lunch with my editor, I accepted. We'll discuss my proposal for the new book and hopefully get a contract.

The elevator car slides down the ten floors and opens at the ground. We're immediately swarmed by a young woman with three small children in tow, and I have to step carefully to avoid getting trampled by a boy with an action figure.

The man who was on the elevator disappears in the direction of the parking garage, but like most New Yorkers, I don't have a car. Instead I head toward the street exit, where I'll take the subway to the publishing house offices.

The same flickering neon latte hangs in front of my favorite coffee shop.

I glance at my phone. There's just enough time to grab a mocha frappe if I hurry. Sure enough, there's no line. I step right up to the counter, where the same barista turns the pages of a science fiction book.

He glances up at me and grins. "You're back."

"It feels so good to be back," I say, which is not entirely a lie. Certain things feel good. Like having an endless stream of boiling hot water for my shower. Wearing my super comfy pajamas to sleep. Other things feel... different. As if I've changed while I've been gone and don't quite fit into my old places. "I'll have my usual."

He nods and turns to begin making my mocha frappe. It's been years of coming here. I don't even know his name; this isn't a nametag kind of place. And he doesn't know mine. But I know what series he's on, and he knows my drink. There's comfort in that.

"So," he says, pouring the syrup in, heavy handed the way I like. "Where did you go? I figured you must've moved away or something."

How to explain? I certainly can't tell the truth. This is a conversation I'll have to have a hundred times—starting at lunch with my agent and editor. "I decided I needed to see the world," I say, which narrowly avoids being a lie. "So I flew to Paris and then took a tour in the countryside. Ended up in Italy, and now I'm home."

He whistles. "Very nice. And impulsive. I hope you don't mind me saying so, but I wouldn't have thought you had it in you."

That makes me laugh. "I didn't think I had it in me, either."

And that part, at least, is the truth. I survived a kidnapping and imprisonment in a French church. I escaped a high-security *appartamente* in Paris. I evaded ex-military forces and confronted an international thug. That's the reason why I don't quite fit into my life here; I've become someone else, someone who can do those things.

Bemused, I pay for my mocha frappe and head outside.

A man sits on the corner stroking a guitar. The sound filters through the bustle and honking.

Sunlight bounces off cars that zoom around each other on the busy street, a rush of yellow taxis and black Ubers. A few delivery trucks and vans break up the color.

From a few streets away I hear shouting. Some kind of parade or maybe a protest. From here they sound the same. A memory rises in my consciousness. Twelve months ago there had been a protest outside the airport in Paris. Shouting that suddenly grew quiet as I rounded a corner.

It seems almost like a dream when the white van careens into my sight. It swerves hard toward the curb. My body knows what's happening before my brain does. I'm already taking a step back. The mocha frappe falls to the ground. The guitar's song ends on a clashing note.

Time slows down.

I can smell the exhaust from the street, the garbage from the sewer. I can feel the hum of the city beneath my feet. I'm turning, running, racing toward the coffee shop. It's become my safe haven in this moment. If I can just make it to the flickering neon latte, I'll escape.

The white van speeds past me and splashes a puddle onto my slacks.

I stand there feeling stupid, so damn stupid. My drink is spilled, the man with the guitar is gaping at me. What's wrong with me? It was twelve months ago that the white van abducted me in Paris. That wouldn't happen to the same girl twice.

The odds would prevent that, wouldn't they?

There's heat behind me. A presence. I turn but time's still slowed down to a crawl. I only have a glimpse of a black SUV, and then something dark covers my face. A hood. I scream, but it's muffled. Hands are firm and careful as they tie my wrists behind my back.

"I'm not going to hurt you," says a voice that sounds familiar.

Alarm streaks through me.

He's lying. He has to be lying, so I strike out with my foot. It connects with hard muscle and bone. There's a muttered curse word, and then I push myself away from his hold. It only succeeds in knocking me against the side of the SUV, and then everything fades away.

CHAPTER TWENTY

HOLLY

MY EYES OPEN to pitch black.

I wait for the room to come into focus. I could be staying anywhere—a farmhouse in France, a penthouse in Italy. Nothing happens. This is the complete kind of darkness, the kind without even shadows. My lungs burn, as if I've been holding my breath. I gulp down damp and moldy air. I curl my fingers against stone. Faintly slick. Gently warm.

Where am I?

Memories drop into my mind like rain in a puddle. I remember the long flight and fear for my sister. I remember the man playing the guitar on the street.

A shudder works its way through my body, lingering in aches and tension, waking up pain as it goes. I move myself to a sitting position with a soft groan. The floor feels slightly uneven, large stone tiles strewn across the floor.

I crawl forward. Something hard meets my face. My fists close around iron bars.

No. *Not again.*

This is a dream. It has to be a dream. Doesn't it?

The darkness closes in on me. It becomes a tactile force, squeezing my lungs. I don't want to stay here, in this pitch-black prison. I can't stay here. There's no oxygen. I gasp through the fist around my throat. I'm going to die here, before anyone can touch me, and that seems almost like a gift, except that the body fights anyway. It wants to live.

"Breathe," comes a voice from the inky void. I choke on air.

"Elijah," I gasp out. It's twisted that I'd actually be relieved to have him here. Anything is better than being alone right now. Even the presence of the man I left behind.

There's quiet.

I'm not alone in the dark, though. My fists curl around iron. "Answer me."

"I'm not Elijah." And he's not. He's missing the rough timbre of Elijah's low voice. His voice is more fluid and slightly accented. I recognize it immediately.

"Adam," I say, wondering. And then again.

"*Adam.*"

I become a force of fury. I fly toward his voice, not even caring if there are iron bars between us. There aren't, there's only air. And I land on him with my fists and my fear. I beat against his strong chest, using it to channel all of this horror.

"How *dare* you," I gasp out. "How dare you keep doing this."

"Calm yourself, ma petite," he says, grasping my wrists in the darkness. "I'm not the one who brought you here. I'm not the one you're angry at."

I'm still struggling, inconsolable. "I don't care. I don't care."

He has the temerity to laugh, a soft chuckle that makes me more angry. "Then beat me until I'm broken. I think I might welcome the pain tonight. It would make the symmetry complete."

"What are you talking about?" I ask, yanking away from him. I stagger backward, tripping over an uneven stone tile, falling to the rough ground.

"Are you all right?"

"No," I say, tears pricking my eyes. God, I don't want to cry in front of him. He won't be able to see me, but he can hear it, sense it. The new Holly is stronger than that. I clench my teeth together and lift my head. "Why did you kidnap me again?"

"I will say it again, though you will not believe me. I did not kidnap you. I'm as much a prisoner as you are, this time around, ma petite."

A match strikes, and flame reaches through the bars. The first thing I see is Adam, disheveled and dirty, leaning against the wall, looking a little worse for the wear. Only next do I look through the iron bars at the man who's holding us here.

The man who abducted me off the New York City streets.

"Hi," I whisper as if we're meeting for the first time.

Elijah gives me a small nod, his voice low and grave. "Hi back."

"What are you doing there?" It's a dumb question. An obvious question. I can't help but ask it because I don't want to imagine the obvious answer.

"I'm exacting a little revenge," he says.

I begin to tremble, even though it's not cold here. Not like France. "Where are we?"

"We're still in New York City."

"You're insane. You can't just do this. You can't just kidnap me here."

"Did you think kidnapping was only permitted in Paris? I could fly you there, of course, but it's so hard to get a bound body through customs."

I stare at the man who's so familiar to me and yet still a stranger. My lover. My enemy. "Elijah. This is insane. Tell me this is a joke."

His head cocks. "Would it be funny to you?"

No. Nothing about this is funny.

The match he holds is small, but it gives off enough light for me to see the room we're in. It's some kind of basement, but more finished than the one underneath the French church. There are elaborate carvings on the wall, sconces empty of candles, and steel bars that look incongruously modern compared to the surroundings.

Symmetry. That was the word Adam used, and I finally understand it. Elijah is wearing a suit. He doesn't look as slick as Adam. He looks strong, instead.

Like a missile encased in bespoke wool.

"Why are you doing this?" I whisper.

"Because you left." He looks away and then back at me, his eyes dark and tragic. "I saw you. I wanted you. And I take what I want. It doesn't have to be more complicated than that, Holly."

"Have you heard of dating?"

He gives me a small, private smile. "This is

better. I don't want to ask you out. I don't want to give you the illusion that you can say no, Holly. You're mine."

"As romantic as this reunion is," Adam says, "might I ask for some water. Food. Bandage. I would even accept medicine."

I glance at him, and my eyes widen. "Is that blood?"

"A bullet wound, I'm afraid," he says, his expression rueful and tight with pain.

"Oh my God," I say, turning back to Elijah. "You shot him."

"It was the only way to compel him into his current state of capture."

"What about your brothers?"

"My brothers." A shadow crosses his eyes. "I love them, but I'm more fully my father than they will ever be. That line they were worried about? I crossed it. It's far behind me now."

The match burns to his fingertips and goes out.

We're cast into darkness. I suck in a breath and step backward, bumping into the warm wall. There must be heaters beneath this building to keep it this way underground. It's a far more comfortable prison than the French church.

What a strange comparison to make. What an

ironic turn in my life. I thought I was returning to my ordinary life with ordinary things. High heels and mocha frappes. Lunch meetings with my agent and editor. What must they be thinking right now? That I'm running late. That I somehow forgot. That I got caught in a subway malfunction, maybe.

They would never imagine that plain Holland Frank would be kidnapped.

They would never imagine this wasn't the first time.

"I'll give you the night to think over your situation," Elijah's voice says through the darkness. "In the morning we'll talk. You'll be more amenable to my demands by then."

"What demands?" I say, panic rising in my throat, my voice squeaking.

His only answer is the click of his dress shoes on stone as he leaves. Hinges make a high-pitched sound. A door closes and locks. We're alone.

I close my eyes, unable to face the reality. Unwilling to face it.

"I'm sorry, ma petite," Adam says.

"For what?"

"For not being able to solve this predicament."

"I'm sorry, too."

"For what?"

"For hitting you when you're already shot."

He gives a small, musical laugh. "That didn't feel amazing, to be sure. But I probably deserved it. And the bullet as well. He was only returning the favor. After all, I shot him first."

I nestle down into the corner, feeling a strange kind of comfort. When you've lived long enough in the dark, it begins to feel like home. "Why did you shoot him?"

"I was his mentor, once. His friend. Then I became indebted to dangerous men. Powerful men. And he became a pawn to his lieutenant colonel. We were soldiers, each of us, on opposite sides of a secret war being waged."

"In other words, he got in your way."

That musical laugh again. "Yes, he got in my way. In my own manner I was trying to help him. Put him out of commission, out of the game. It wasn't a lethal wound."

"Neither was yours, it seems."

"No, apparently our friend has a strong sense of symmetry."

My chest constricts. He said he'll make demands of us tomorrow. "How far do you think he'll go to maintain that symmetry? Do you think he would make us... kiss?"

"I have come to regret those games," he says. "They weren't respectful."

Anger wells in my heart. "You play the games. He plays the games. And always, I'm in the middle of them. Why? I'm just a regular girl."

"I chose you before because you were the one thing he wanted but couldn't have."

"But I'm nothing to you."

"Nothing? No. I've come to care about what happens to you, but you aren't my lost love. That's where he broke the symmetry. If he'd wanted to pick the one thing I wanted but couldn't have, there would be someone else sitting in this cell with me."

Because we're whispering confidences, I ask, "Who?"

"Someone you know," he surprises me by saying. "Someone you love."

My forehead knits. "But who—"

"It does not matter. What matters is that clearly he plans to exact his revenge tomorrow. We had better rest and get some sleep."

"I'm not going to sleep," I say. "Now tell me who this person is. We barely know the same people. I can't think of anyone who—No. Not London."

"Is it so hard to believe? I imagine many men

fall in love with her every day. The irony is that I have Elijah to thank for meeting her. If he hadn't slipped her the diamonds, I would never have met her."

"You're the one who helped her," I realize. "The one who helped me escape Paris."

"Yes."

"Because you wanted her to love you back?"

"God, no. She has no business being with someone like me. In the same way you have no business being with someone like Elijah North. When men like us sell our souls to the devil, there's nothing left to give to a woman."

CHAPTER TWENTY-ONE

ELIJAH

O F COURSE I don't go to sleep.

There are infrared cameras set up in the basement, and I seat myself on one of the pews. The pulpit is quiet and dark. Even this many years later there's the faint scent of incense. It's embedded in the wood and thin wool carpet.

The church has been abandoned for a few years now. I bought the property under a shell company for twenty thousand dollars at a public auction.

It makes a good safe house.

Even my brothers don't know about it.

Thinking of them makes my jaw clench. There's no going back now. They would never accept me again after what I've done, but this is who I am. It was always a false front that they welcomed into their fold. They thought I was like them. I'm not.

I'm like our father.

I pull up the camera, and of course, *of course*, they're talking.

Adam is always fucking talking, and Holly is too curious for her own good. It pisses me off, even as I acknowledge that I created this situation. Maybe I even created it to force them to talk, because I'm a perverse son of a bitch.

"When men like us sell our souls to the devil, there's nothing left to give to a woman." Damn the man for telling the truth. There's nothing left in my soul but darkness and violence. That's what I'm showing her by taking her captive. She left because I couldn't give her empty promises—now I'm showing her exactly why they would have been empty.

"Bullshit," she says, her voice calm and clear over the speaker. "That's an excuse men like you use to keep from feeling anything, because emotions are more scary than bullets."

Soft laughter. "I see why Elijah likes you so much."

"Yes," she says, her voice dry. "He likes me so much he kidnapped me."

"He's trying to prove a point."

"What point?"

"That he doesn't deserve you."

That's the problem with making an enemy of

a man you once called a friend. He knows me too well. Of course I don't deserve Holly. Now she'll finally see that.

They grow quiet after that.

Holly wanders the edges of her prison in much the same way she wandered the edges of the crypt under the French church. She's a woman who always needs to test her boundaries. That's one of the things I admire. And it's one of the reasons we can never be together.

I'm a man who will always put cages around her.

In the back there are two cots with thin pallets on top. Ironically it's more comfortable than the hard wooden pew that will be my mattress tonight.

She curls up on her side facing the wall, as if she knows I have a camera, as if she doesn't want me to know she's crying. I hear her sniffles anyway. Each one is a stake to the heart.

I leave the laptop running on the ground as I recline on the pew. Rafters weave an intricate pattern beneath the roof of the church. Evening light passes through dirt-smudged stained glass windows. Smudges of green and purple and pink wander across the plaster walls.

Dreams lap at my feet, a respite I haven't had

since I returned to the villa and discovered Holly missing. I haven't been able to sleep. I've barely been able to eat.

Now she's under my control again, and I can finally breathe.

When I open my eyes, night has fallen.

It looked almost pretty in the twilight, even derelict and abandoned. Now darkness encroaches on every surface. Now the church looks as vacant as the open eyes of a corpse.

A plastic bag waits for me at the end of the pew. I pick it up. There's a few bottles of water inside. Some alcohol swabs and bandages.

I carry it downstairs.

Adam is already waiting by the bars, standing between me and Holly as if he can protect her from me. The idea makes me laugh; the sound echoes in the basement. I'm the one with the gun. He's the one with a bullet in his chest.

"Are you going to be her knight in shining armor?" I ask, my voice casual.

He curls each fist around a bar. "Will you make me?"

I hold up the bag. "Supplies. Water. I even threw in a few candy bars."

Holly appears behind Adam, her face drawn and pale. She puts her hands around her arms, but it doesn't completely hide her shiver. Even with the heaters I had installed, it would be cold down here. "What do we have to do to get them?"

My voice becomes sardonic. "This is too easy. Aren't you going to argue with me first? Aren't you going to beg like you did in France? You beg so pretty, Holly."

The taunts have the desired effect. She firms her lips. Anger flashes across her dark eyes. She even looks taller as her spine straightens. "You're a bastard."

"Is that any way to speak to your captor?"

"Go to hell."

I make a *tsk* sound. "Your cellmate needs the bandages in this bag. So even if you aren't thirsty, and I'm sure by now that you are, you might do it for him."

"And what exactly do I have to do?"

"Kiss him, of course. My little brown-haired Barbie and Interpol Ken. What else will I do with you while I have you here in my pretend mansion?"

Hurt flashes over her face before she hides it behind anger. "You want to see me kiss him? You arranged this whole thing so you could get a little soft-core porn? Fine."

That's my only warning before she turns Adam around and lifts up on her toes. She presses her lips to his in a clumsy kiss, and jealousy surges inside my chest. She fought my kiss. She recoiled from it, but she's kissing this man—and he's kissing her back.

He may have a thing for London, but he has no problem kissing her sister. He cups the back of her head and leans over her. His lips tease hers, the motion at once sweet and explicit.

My stomach turns over. I hate the sight of them together. It feels wrong and dangerous, but I'm free-falling from a high altitude. The only way to go is down.

"Make her come." My voice comes out hoarse.

Adam doesn't even stop kissing her. He moans his assent. I watch Holly stiffen. She's alarmed, but it will only make her hotter. She likes it when she fights.

I do, too. My mind may know this is wrong, but my body has no problem with the picture playing out in front of me. My hard cock presses against my suit.

He flips her around, and she grasps the bars to remain upright.

His hands roam her body, pinching her breasts, smoothing over her stomach. He cups her pussy over the cute little black skirt she wears.

Her eyes are wide as she watches me, and nothing, absolutely nothing can hide the lust that lurks in their depths. She likes this. She hates it. It fucking turns her on.

Adam murmurs in her ear. "See the way he watches you? He can't look away. He wants his hands to be on your sweet body. He wants to feel how wet you are."

Some small part of me recognizes that I'm losing my control of the situation, but most of me doesn't care. She looks so fucking hot, her hips rocking forward, seeking more pressure from Adam, her head tilting back onto his shoulder.

I love watching this woman's pleasure, even if another man gives it to her.

"No," she moans.

"Yes," I say, stepping forward, shoving my hand through the bars, gripping her chin so she's forced to face me. "You came so hard this way. I think you like it rough, sweetheart."

She shakes her head, but it's useless, useless when she's making those breathy little whimpers. Adam rubs her clit with the heel of his hand. It's a crude way to make her come. Nothing like a good finger fuck. Nothing like licking her until she creams.

She's not even undressed, but she humps his hand, desperate, hungry.

"Stop," I say, my voice hard as steel.

CHAPTER TWENTY-TWO

HOLLY

T HE PRESSURE DISAPPEARS, and I want to cry. It felt so good, as if I were floating on a cloud. There were no bars, no cots. No bags of water bottles. Only pleasure.

Now it's gone.

I whimper my dismay. "Please," I beg, beyond caring.

My hips rock forward against the bars, and I can't imagine how I look right now. Elijah stands there like a fortress in a suit—impenetrable. Adam's hand may have played with me, but Elijah is the one who controlled the strings. "Please," I say again.

His green eyes look past me. "You. Back the fuck off."

The heat from Adam melts away. Then it's only the two of us standing a foot apart, cold metal bars between us, an entire world between us.

We'll never be on the same side again.

I know this is wrong and perverse, but somehow that only makes me hotter. There are two men watching me, two men burning for me. I don't need to look down at the erections between their legs to know this. It's clear in their eyes.

I glance back at Adam, and he's lounging on the cot, a pair of slitted eyes.

Elijah taps my clit through the fabric. "Look at me."

And so I look into his green, green eyes. They look like the glittering surface of the sea, and I feel a pang of regret for ever leaving that paradise. If I had never run from him, I would never know the depths he would go to catch me.

He pushes the heel of his hand against my clit. "Go on. Make yourself feel good, sweetheart."

My cheeks burn, but I obey him. I rock my hips against his hand using the bars for leverage. His gaze never leaves mine, not even when I climb onto the precipice, not even when I fall. The orgasm clenches every muscle in my body, and I keen my perverse pleasure.

There is no time to relax after the climax. I wrench myself away from the bars.

"I hate you," I say between gritted teeth. Tears of humiliation dampen my cheeks.

"That's fine, sweetheart." Elijah doesn't sound bothered in the least. He scrubs his hand over his face, the same hand he used to make me come. He breathes deep as if enjoying the scent of me. It feels primal, having my scent on him, and I fight the satisfaction it gives me.

"Why are you doing this?"

"Because I can."

"Adam thinks you're trying to prove a point. That you don't deserve me."

An eyebrow rises. "Do you think I deserve you?"

"At this point you only deserve a hard kick between the legs."

He laughs, revealing white teeth. Why does he have to look so handsome? As good as he looks in a T-shirt and tactical pants, he somehow looks even better in a suit. His green eyes sparkle. "I've always liked that violent edge you hide from the world."

"You bring it out in me."

He crouches in front of the bars. "Fine. Here's a real answer. Because this is who I really am. You met me in captivity last year. I was injured and beaten. Tortured. Hungry. So you assumed I was tame. That wasn't true then, and it definitely isn't true now."

Tame? No, he's definitely a wild animal. Feral. "You're angry at Adam. You should be. He shot you and imprisoned you, but I didn't do any of that. So why am I here?"

"For the same reason a lion drags a lioness into his den."

I shiver, and though I hide my response, my body heats. This particular lioness likes to be dragged around by her lion. "I will fight you."

"Good." He pushes the bag through the bars. "You earned this."

Humiliation threatens to drive me to my knees. My stomach turns over, but I force myself to face him with my head held high. He created this situation. He's responsible for every ounce of shame it causes me.

Not that it bothers him much.

He gives me a small smile, not abashed in the least. He turns and walks away, sure of my response. Sure that my desperation will make me comply.

It's with shaking hands that I sort through the offering he brought. I need the water, and I know that in a few hours, I'll be grateful for a Snickers bar. Except that's what he wants from me. That will only give me enough strength to play more of his sick games.

He wants to prove that he's evil? Let him.

I shove the bag back to him. It slides through the bars, beyond my reach.

He stops and turns back around. "What are you doing?"

"Fighting you."

He looks pitying. "That's only going to make you weaker."

"Yes. It will kill me if you wait too long."

"So you think I'm going to release you if you don't eat."

"Or drink. Yes. I don't think you're as terrible as you want me to believe. I don't believe you'd let an innocent woman starve to death. That's something your father might have done, but you're not like him. No matter what you say."

Shadows flicker through his green eyes, and I have the sense that he isn't fully in the present. Memories are dragging him back. They may even claim him for good. It's a war I'm fighting. For the man inside him who wants to be honorable.

I believe he's there, even if Elijah doesn't.

He turns and leaves the basement.

My throat constricts as if to remind me how thirsty I am. The bag of water sits a couple yards away from the bars. Far enough that I can't reach it, but I can look at it.

When I look back, Adam is looking at me with a mixture of amusement and dismay. "Hell," he says. "You might have consulted me first."

Guilt gnaws at my insides. "I'm so sorry. And you're injured."

He laughs. "It was worth it to see the shock on his face. He didn't see that coming. And don't worry. I'll live. If only to spite Elijah North, I'm making it out of this cell."

I curl up on my cot and fall into a deep sleep of exhaustion.

Dreams come in the form of an endless black ocean. I'm falling, crashing into the water. The impact leaves me breathless. Water swirls around me. Bubbles escape my lips.

When I can finally see, there are nets all around me. Beside me, beneath me.

Even above me, keeping me from the surface.

The nets pull tighter and tighter, until they trap my arms against my body. They wrap tight around my tail so I can't swim anymore, and then I'm falling, sinking into the black abyss.

CHAPTER TWENTY-THREE

ADAM

APPARENTLY I'M ON a hunger strike.

It wouldn't have been my choice, especially with the bleeding coming from my side, but I'll stand in solidarity with Holly. Or sit, which may be my only option. Lying down also works.

Holly is sleeping so deeply that she didn't stir even when I used the bucket in the back corner, thank God for small favors. Now she has a gentle snore that somehow sounds cute.

There's a creak at the top of the stairs, but she doesn't move. I stand and move between her and the stairs, ignoring the throb in my side. It's ridiculous, really, the idea that I could protect her. A hard wind would knock me over. Now I understand why Elijah was intent on defending her in that French church.

Holly Frank has a way of bringing out the protective instinct in a man.

Elijah has shed his suit jacket upstairs. He's

wearing shirtsleeves rolled up and rumpled. That doesn't make him look nearly as casual as his socks. Black dress socks. He's not wearing any shoes. It's like he got drunk on the sacramental wine and then came downstairs.

Which is a real possibility.

He stands a few feet away from the bars. Far enough that I can't lunge for him. Smart man. Even with a bullet in my side it wouldn't stop me from trying.

"Have you come to play more games?" I ask, my voice polite.

He nods, his eyes a dark and stormy sea.

That makes me laugh. "How far are you going to take this? Or haven't you thought that far out? Will you make me finger fuck her? Eat her out? Are you really going to stand there and watch as I fuck the woman you love?"

"I don't love her." *I don't love anyone*, comes the unspoken corollary.

"You're going to lose her."

"She's already lost."

"Christ." I shake my head. "When I met you, you were just a stupid kid intent on getting himself killed. Now we meet again all these years later, and you are the same."

"Spare me the French accent."

"So you know my true identity." He doesn't just know my true identity. He lives it. Which means I need to leave this goddamn cell. I need to leave New York City. Because wherever Elijah North is, Lieutenant Colonel Mark Jefferson isn't far behind. "And I know yours. Do you think we didn't run a background check? The good kind. Not whatever you put on the form when you enlisted."

"Stop."

"Seeing your mother killed when you were three, that had to be hard."

He takes a step closer to the bars. "I said, stop."

"Being beat to shit by the same man who killed her, every goddamn day, that must have been hard. Watching your brothers leave, one by one. They abandoned you."

"I don't blame them."

"You should. They're not the heroes you think they are."

"I've done things—"

"You killed your father."

"You think I regret that? You think I fucking regret it? I waited years to do that. Too many years. That's the thing, you always assumed I regretted that part, but the only thing I regretted was waiting so long. I'm a murderer, Adam. A proud one."

"If you're so proud of what you've done, why can't you be with her?"

He glances at her. The faint light from the top of the stairs shines a halo around her dark head. The soft sounds of her snores continue. "If you did a real background check, then you know what wasn't on the forms. Any mention of me between age fourteen and eighteen."

My chest constricts, and I force myself to continue breathing evenly. He can hear it, he can sense it, and if he feels even an ounce of pity, he'll leave. "A runaway."

"Running implies someone was looking for me. No one looked."

"No one cared."

He gives me a sardonic glance. "Are you trying to be my therapist?"

I look up at the ceiling. "Or maybe a priest. Do you have a confession to make?"

"Yeah," he says, his voice low and thoughtful. "I thought my brothers were heroes. I wanted to be like them. I guess some part of me still does. I thought you were a hero, too."

"Then you met me in France, and you discovered I was just a dirty bastard."

"Same as everyone else."

"That why you tried to steal the diamonds?"

"I stole them for my country, because my commanding officer asked me to. It was a shitty reason, of course. Greed. The same reason your COs wanted them."

"So does that make us corrupt or our commanding officers?"

"I think it makes the government corrupt."

"We're all fucking dirty."

He glances at Holly again. "Not all of us."

"This runaway. What did he do to survive?" I keep my voice light. There is no weight whatsoever given to sympathy. No heaviness around the idea of shame.

"The same thing everyone else had to do." He stares at me as if willing me to understand. Or maybe he really does want me to absolve him. "I dealt drugs when I could."

"And when you couldn't?"

He looks away this time. "It was a long time ago."

"It still haunts you."

"Why shouldn't it? I'm unclean. I never should have touched Holly Frank. You never should have made me touch her in that French prison."

"It's one of the few things in my life I don't regret doing."

He glares at me. "I should shoot you again."

I look down at the dark stain of blood on my gray T-shirt. "A graze, really. About the same place where I shot you, almost to the inch. As if you didn't really want me to die."

"I could say the same about you."

I smile. "So what's it going to be? Should I fuck her ass? Maybe tie her up, introduce her to the pleasures of a flogger?"

"Hell."

"How far will you go, Elijah North?"

"You want to know what line I won't cross?"

"We both know you aren't going to let her starve to death."

"Do we know that?"

"I don't even think you'd let me die. If I collapsed right now, you'd probably call an ambulance."

He gives me a dark look. "I wouldn't test that theory."

"Where is the line, Elijah?"

"Way back in the distance. I passed it a long time ago."

"Then you won't mind if I wake her up right now. You won't mind if I kiss her, if I touch her,

If I fuck her. Right? You already crossed the fucking line, is that right?"

He stares at me, and for a moment I think he's going to call my bluff.

Then he swears under his breath. "You are so determined to be my mentor."

"When you stop needing one, I'll stop being one."

"Spare me the zen bullshit." He tosses me something through the bars. I catch a single key. "You can walk yourself back to Brooklyn. Or crawl. I don't care."

"Shouldn't you provide a ride?"

"I had to rough it through the goddamn French countryside. I had to catch us a couple of dormice to eat before we found shelter. You can manage the Lowest East Side."

"Fair." I regard the key with suspicion. I may have been willing to mouth off to the man from behind the bars. Prisoners have very little to lose. That doesn't mean I'm taking my safety for granted. It wouldn't make sense to turn your back on a tiger. "This is real?"

"Oh, it'll open the door all right." He gives a shrug. "As to whether I'll shoot you in the back, you'll have to find that one out the hard way."

CHAPTER TWENTY-FOUR
ELIJAH

HOLLY MUST HAVE been exhausted. I suppose abject terror can do that.

She sleeps for another two hours while I keep watch over her.

I know when she wakes because of the stillness in the air. And because she stops that soft snore. It becomes quiet in the room, with only her stormy thoughts to fill the space.

"Do you think he'll come back soon?" she asks without turning her head, and I realize that she thinks I'm Adam. She can probably sense my presence, but she assumes I'm him.

I don't answer, because I want to prolong the time it takes her to discover me. She won't be pleased to see me. That's the irony. That I wanted to punish Adam but really I just made him a hero. I'm the villain in her story.

"When he does, I think we should accept the water and medicine," she says. "I shouldn't have refused like that, not when you need it more than I do."

And still I say nothing.

Her voice comes softer this time, more reflective. "Do you think he would let you go if I promised to do what he said? That way you could see a doctor. Do you think he'd make that trade?"

"It's a good idea," I say. "I wish I'd thought of it."

She scrambles up in the bed and backs up to the wall. "Elijah."

"That's me."

"What are you doing here? Where's Adam?"

A pang in my chest. "Do you miss him? You seem pretty worried about him."

"He's been *shot*. By you."

"Well, don't worry about him anymore, sweetheart. He's free of this hellhole. There's only you and me. And you didn't even make a promise to obey me. That means you're free to fight when I fuck you, pretend like you don't want what I'm giving you."

"How dare you."

"I know you like it better when you fight."

She could have withdrawn when I taunted her. She could have started crying. There would have been nothing left for me to do but take her back to her pretty little loft in her pretty little building. She could have brunch with mimosas and avocado toast. Yeah, I studied her staid life. The life that she thinks suits her.

Instead she lifts her chin. "Whatever I may have liked, that was in the past. Before you freaking abducted me. Off the street."

"Would you prefer I abduct you from the terrace of the restaurant with your editor and agent looking on? Or maybe you'd like it better if I'd stolen into your loft at night, if I'd appeared in your bed with a ski mask and masking tape for your wrists?"

She tries to look furious. She really fucking tries. But the way her cheeks darken is clear to me from a few feet away. The way her eyes brighten with lust makes my cock hard.

There's no hiding from me.

I stand and dust my hands off. This will be fun. "How about this? You can pretend you're disgusted with me when I make you come so hard you see God. You can scream and cry and faint when I lick your pretty little pussy."

"I won't like it. I won't."

I notice that she doesn't deny it's going to happen. She knows that we're going to fuck. Her body's already preparing itself for me. Her pussy would be wet if I touched it.

She glances at the door to the cell. It's open an inch.

"Don't," I warn her. "Remember what I told you in Italy. Running only makes me chase you. It only makes me pin you down and fuck even harder as punishment."

She broadcasts her decision seconds before she actually bolts for the door. I could catch her right away, but I let her scramble to the door. It's more fun to press her against the iron bars. More fun to push my body against her so she can feel my erection.

She goes still at the feel. "That was before."

"Before I took you captive? Make no mistake, sweetheart. You were mine from the moment your pretty little ass landed in that French church."

"No," she whispers.

Carefully, very carefully, I lift her hair away. And I place a soft kiss at the back of her neck. Then I use teeth, scraping against the same place that I kissed. Gentleness and force. I'll always be a mixture of the two where she's concerned. "Yes."

She bucks her hips, trying to push me off. All it does is send friction through my cock.

I push back, grinding hard enough to make

her whimper.

The gentleness part of the night is over. There's only force now. I reach around through the bars and feel her breasts pressed against iron. The contrast of soft and hard makes me groan. "You're so pretty," I murmur. "But I like you better in the dark."

There's only the two of us in the dark. The world fades away.

"I'm going to cross the line. Again and again," I murmur against her hair. "You have to be the one to stop me. You have to make me stop, understand?"

"What if I can't?"

"You have to draw the line. I need you to do that." I'm forcing her, and I'm begging at the same time. I need her to draw the line because lord knows I can't draw it myself.

"What if I won't?"

Frustration rises in me, along with a swelling of lust. The beast inside me likes the idea of there being no line. No barriers. The man is sure that I'll take it too far. "A person should have a line," I tell her. "That's your fucking job here."

CHAPTER TWENTY-FIVE

HOLLY

I'M FURIOUS AT Elijah for abducting me. I'm relieved that he did.

The contradiction is tearing me apart.

"I hate you," I say on a whisper, and that's not a lie.

He bites my neck again, and then the junction of my shoulder, and then my back. He leaves his teeth marks all over me like a brand, and I arch my back from the pure pleasure of it.

I turn around in his arms. If I'm an animal in captivity, then I can bite back. I bite his chin, his jaw. I bite the soft flesh of his lower lip until he grunts in pain.

Something metallic drops on my tongue. Blood.

Such a small thing, but it makes me relent. Now that I've hurt him, I can relax in his arms. "I love you," I say on a whisper, and that's not a lie either.

He shoves the pleated skirt up to my waist. He pushes the placket of my panties aside, and then he's inside me, thrusting hard into a body not quite ready. He's too large, and I squirm to get away. The thickness feels like an invasion. It feels like something I need to fight.

But he doesn't relent. He's merciless as he fucks me into the bars, his arms holding me beneath my thighs, his body impelling me against the iron. There might be grid-shaped bruises on my back when we're done, and the thought of it makes me moan.

My orgasm comes as hard and violent as the way he fucks me. It rolls over my body in clenching waves, and I scream against his shoulder. He rocks through the climax, making it last until every ounce of breath has been wrung out of me. I'm gasping for air when he finally slows down. Then he lets me go and I slide bonelessly down his body.

Only when I'm kneeling at his feet does he grasp his cock.

His hand moves in a blur. He fucks his fist in front of my face, and it's pure instinct that has me opening my mouth. He grips the base of his cock and presses the tip to my lips. I suck him, made hungry by some primal motive, pushing my face against his body, letting him invade my throat. I swallow around him, and he comes with a roar that bounces off the stone walls.

He seems to come forever, spilling salt onto my tongue, making me gasp for air.

"Clean me," he says, his green eyes almost demonic as he looks down on me. Or maybe holy. Either way I know to obey him, and I lick the come around the crown of his cock. *A person should have a line,* he told me, but I run my tongue along the vein underneath.

My knees are clenched together from arousal, and he bends down and pries them apart. *You have to draw the line. I need you to do that.* Then his mouth is between my legs, my black pleated skirt up around my waist. His tongue strokes my clit over and over again, endless, relentless, and I beg. "No, please, wait."

He doesn't stop. He doesn't wait. He only licks me until tears stream down my cheeks. I push myself backwards to get away, but the bars imprison me. Even now, in this intimate moment, he conspires to kidnap me. *I'm going to cross the line. Again and again.* I want him to cross it. He forces two fingers inside me, and I sob from the hard invasion. He rubs in a cruel, cruel pattern. One designed to push me over the edge. This time when I come it's a quick flash in the dark, an explosion that leaves my ears ringing.

We both collapse onto the hard, dusty floor, panting, our breaths loud in the hollow room. Reality returns to me in cold, shocking flashes: the disarray of my clothes, the cell door open that crucial inch, the fact that Adam is no longer here.

"Hi," he says.

It makes me smile. "Hi back."

"What the hell did the lieutenant colonel say to you?"

"Nothing."

He gives me a dark look. "I can imagine him coming in with all his self-righteous bluster, his arguments and his threats. What I can't understand is why you listened to him."

"He said he was going to try you for treason."

"Fuck treason. That's not why you left before I could even say goodbye."

"Would you have said goodbye if I'd waited?"

"Hell no."

"Then that's why I left."

"Something he said spooked you."

"I was worried, all right? I was worried that I would crush the life out of you. We come from such different worlds. I go to brunch and you *kidnap* me. I could never survive in your world, and what if…" A tear trickles down my cheek. "What if you can't survive in mine, either?"

His jaw works. "I don't know, Holly."

"That's why I left without seeing you. He said it would crush the life out of you, trying to fit with me, and I didn't want to be responsible for that."

"Hell. I love you."

Another woman might have been moved to happiness by hearing the confession. I burst into tears. "Don't. Don't. You don't love me."

"Do you think I chose this? Do you think it matters what I want? My love for you is irrational. It defies logic and reason and common sense, but that's what makes it love. We aren't convenient, Holly. We don't fit, but I can't live without you. That's what makes it love."

"What if love isn't enough?"

"Enough for what? I'm going to be with you if I have to tear down every goddamn door in my path, if I have to abduct you from a hundred street corners."

"He said he'll charge you with treason, Elijah."

"Every relationship has problems."

"This is serious."

He scrubs a hand over his face. "I know. I

don't give a shit that he's going to smear my name through the mud, but it means you can't live in your loft with your sad-looking succulents."

"You were inside my loft?"

"And worse, it means I can't involve my brothers. Even knowing me will taint them, but I can't make it worse by asking for their help. When I go on the run, I do it without them." His expression turns grave. "The only question left is whether I do it alone."

CHAPTER TWENTY-SIX

ELIJAH

W E LEAVE THE church in the same black SUV that we arrived in.

Except this time there's no dark hood over Holly's head. No duct tape on her wrists. We're both in the front this time, me on the driver's side, her in the passenger seat. My hand plays with her fingers, linking them together, stroking the sensitive places on her palm.

Maybe this is what she meant by dating.

It's a foreign idea.

Not an entirely unpleasant one.

Her head's turned away from me. She watches the city go by.

"What's wrong?" I ask.

She shakes her head, which just confirms my suspicion.

I squeeze her hand gently. "Tell me, sweetheart. Or I'll force the answer out of you. You probably won't enjoy that process, but I definitely will."

A pretty pink blush covers her cheeks. "He told me he would have the charges of treason dropped if I left you alone." She glares at me, but it's overshadowed by her worry. "But he said our deal was off if you found me again."

Loving someone is hell. I want to slay dragons for her. Instead there's only one dragon, and he's a bastard with the weight of the US government behind him. "I'm thinking."

Panic darkens her brown eyes. "You can drop me off at my loft. You don't have to come in. We can pretend like you never found me again."

"Pretend like I never fucked you against the bars beneath a New York City church? Pretend like you didn't scream and beg and cry when you came? No fucking way."

"There are more important things than sex."

"I can't think of any."

"Your *life*."

"He's not going to kill me. I'm too valuable." Unfortunately Holly is the leverage he needs, which means she's in more danger than ever before. It seems he already suspected that when he visited her in Italy. Following her to New York City confirms it for him.

That's a problem, but it's not going to keep

me from her. Nothing will.

"There's something else," she says, then looks away again. "Another reason we can't be together. A more important one."

I wish I wasn't driving, so I could take her chin between my thumb and forefinger, so I could make her look at me. Instead I grip the steering wheel until it creaks in protest. "What?"

"He said he understands you better than I ever will."

"The man can't understand a basic requisition form."

"He said you need the work he's offering you."

Hell. The man actually had found my sore spot, my constant need for danger. The adrenaline rush, the violence. It's the only thing I know. "I can do that work with my brothers."

"Not if you're wanted for treason."

No, not if I'm wanted for treason. I'm useless to my brothers like this. And my hands are tied. The best thing I can do is stay under the radar. Any sort of exposure would only draw attention to me. Even a bar fight could lead to death and discovery. "I'll take up knitting."

"He said I'd only strangle the life out of you." Her voice becomes a whisper. "And he's right.

That's why I left Italy. A person should have a line, you said, and you're right. That's my line. I refuse to strangle the life out of you. Because I love you too much to do that."

I swerve the SUV and pull over in an alley. That way I can grasp her face on either side and look her in the eye. That way I can snarl at her, a lion being denied his mate. "Then love me more than that. Love me enough to ruin my fucking life."

She gives a watery laugh. "You're insane."

The alleyway has the faint smell of kung pao chicken. There's a dumpster, and beyond that, a structure made of cardboard boxes and milk crates that probably houses a homeless person. It makes a more appropriate confessional than the church.

It's the kind of place I lived in until I enlisted.

"You trusted me enough to tell me this. I need to trust you the same way." I swallow hard. "You need to know the kind of man you're entrusting your life with."

She turns to me, her expression earnest. "I can fight, you know. You don't always have to protect me. And I already figured out that I can write on the run."

She's worried about fitting into my life, and the idea cracks the cold metal fortress around my heart. "Listen. I'm not worried about you being strong enough. You're a goddess."

Her expression turns abashed. "Then what were you going to tell me?"

"What happened to me after I left my father's house. Or what I became. It's not really about the things that were done to me. My father beat me, and it was never really part of me. But after I left, the things I did to survive, they're burned into my soul."

"You don't have to tell me what you did."

"But I do." I run a hand over my face. "The truth is it will be a hard road trying to negotiate a peace with the lieutenant colonel. We'll be hiding until I can work out a strategy. Gather the right leverage. You need to know who you're hiding with."

"I already know you."

"No. You know the man I am now. The soldier."

Her eyes turn soft. "Who were you then? Before the soldier?"

"I was a whore." The word comes out hard and flat. There's no sugarcoating that reality. There's no pretending it's anything other than disgusting. "I dealt drugs, but when I couldn't, when I needed cash, when I needed food, I knew the right street corner. It wasn't so different than this one. Wait until someone drives by and rolls down the window. Give him a price."

Her eyes are wide. She doesn't look horrified, but that's because she's busy being shocked out of her mind. I looked up the house where Liam left her. White fence, vegetable garden. It's an entire world apart from the ramshackle mobile home I grew up. A different planet entirely than the makeshift structure a few yards in front of us. I slept in a place like that. I know how little it does to keep out the cold and rain. I know about the rats and the roaches.

"Oh, Elijah," she whispers. "No."

Grief. That's the first idea that comes into my head. The first stage of grief is denial. What is she grieving, then? Her love for me? Ruined. Our life together? Gone.

"Yes," I say, my voice grim. There should be no doubt.

"And you feel shame for that. Of course you do," she says, almost to herself. "Your father failed you. The system failed you, but you blame yourself."

"My father was a bastard, but he had nothing to do with me after I left."

"Nothing to do with you? He beat you until

you had no other choice but to leave."

And there is anger. Pretty soon she'll come to accept the reason we can't be together. I'm not a man who any woman could love, not when she knows the truth about me.

Her eyes turn fierce. "How dare you."

Shame thumps hard in my chest. "I should have told you. I know that."

"*Then love me more than that,*" she says, mocking me. "*Love me enough to ruin my fucking life.*"

"That was before you knew. I won't hold you to that."

"You're determined to break my heart." Tears fill her eyes. "You beautiful, brave, *stupid* man. You want me to love you? I already do. Telling me something that hurt you in the past will never change that. Telling me what you did to survive? Do you think I'd rather you starved?"

"I starved you," I tell her, my voice grim. "No food. No water."

"That's not precisely true. You offered it. And I turned it down." She gives me an impish look. "Besides the fact that you only kept me captive overnight."

"I don't think many women would be so understanding of being held captive for any time period."

"Everything you did, everything you survived, it only brought you to me. Understand?" She holds my face the same way I held hers. I can't tear my gaze away. "I would take away your pain if I could, but the only thing I can do now is promise that you'll never be alone again."

There's a distinct tear. That's what it feels like in my chest. Something ripping into shreds. That old blanket of shame, perhaps. I make a rough groan and press my lips to hers. It's a messy kiss. There's nothing slow or sensual about it. It's a mashing of lips. A claiming.

"Come on," I murmur against her lips. "Let's get your things."

I start up the SUV again and maneuver into the flow of traffic. One conversation cannot erase a lifetime of shame. One conversation cannot assuage my guilt over derailing her life.

It's a start.

She's the one who stepped out of the church. Instead it feels like I'm the one who finally left my self-imposed prison. It feels like I'm the one warmed by sunlight for the first time in years.

It feels like hope.

At least until we step inside her loft.

The lieutenant colonel sits in her favorite armchair for writing. He's flanked by two men in uniform who look ready to shoot us on sight. The lieutenant colonel smiles. "There you are. You've kept me waiting, but I won't hold that against you. Sit, sit."

CHAPTER TWENTY-SEVEN

HOLLY

IT'S EASY TO think of Elijah North as invincible.

Only when he's naked and underneath me, brought low by desire, made weak by how much he needs me, can I really see that he's flesh and blood. A man.

Which means he can be shot. Hurt. Killed. Even as my mind rebels against that idea, my body pumps blood fast and hard. I'm preparing for combat. I may not be a soldier the way that Elijah is, the way these men on either side of the lieutenant colonel are, but I'm a fighter.

"Good afternoon," Elijah says, his voice casual and sardonic, as if he isn't surprised. The only thing that betrays his shock is his stillness. "Sir."

"I see you haven't lost your manners. Though I think we should disarm you to make sure."

There's a moment of taut silence. Then Elijah moves with deliberate slowness, taking a gun from his ankle holster and a knife from his pocket. He sets them down on the foyer table alongside a vase of fake calla lilies.

"One more," the lieutenant colonel says, and Elijah produces another compact gun.

He sets it down and stands with his hands at his side. I have to peer around him to see the lieutenant colonel, and I realize that he's blocking me with his body. He's using himself as a shield to protect me in case someone starts shooting. And I'm close enough to the door that maybe I could even escape, however unlikely.

If I were willing to leave him behind.

If I were willing to sacrifice him to save myself.

Elijah lifts his hands. "What now?"

"Now we talk," the lieutenant colonel says. "I did warn the girl what would happen if you found her again. I thought it wasn't likely, though. I thought you were smarter than that."

"Nope," Elijah says. "Dumb as a rock. Makes me wonder why you want me to work for you. Seems like you have enough dumb fuckers under your command already."

"Elijah, Elijah. You always were the best. Much better than Adam."

"Adam?" I ask before I can stop myself. He's been inextricably linked to Elijah for the entire time I've known him, but I know there's more to the story.

"Yes," the lieutenant colonel says. "Though he always took after his bitch of a mother more than me. She was a spy, you see. I thought I was getting a nice, obedient mail-order bride. Instead I got one of Russia's finest."

Shock leaves me rooted to the floor. "He's your son?"

"My one and only. I would have preferred if our Elijah here were my child." He grants him a fond look that feels more creepy than paternal. "We have much more in common."

"No, you don't," I say.

"Of course we do. Both of us are coldhearted sons of bitches with a talent for killing people. Neither of us care much what flag we do it under." His expression turns cold. "And both of us have a weakness when it comes to sweet pussy."

I shiver at the crude description. And the way it does seem to apply to Elijah. Only the dark side of him. There is another side, one that's held me, cradled me. Protected me. "You're wrong."

"Don't bother," Elijah murmurs. "It doesn't matter what he thinks. The only thing that matters is that we make a deal with him."

"Deals require leverage," the lieutenant colonel says. "You don't have any."

"No? I think some members of the US government would be very interested to know about some of the shadow operations you've conducted. Some against its own citizens."

"Those operations would implicate you as much as me." The lieutenant colonel breathes harder, and his eyes take on a harsh beady gleam. Certainty washes over me; he'll never leave Elijah North alone. He'll never stop following him. Never stop hounding him. Elijah had more freedom trapped in that French church than he does anywhere else. He'll never be free.

"Mutually assured destruction."

"I could blame you completely. Nothing was ever in writing."

"Mostly because you can't write a form with complete fucking sentences. The good news is that I recorded some of our conversations. Senators who conveniently disappeared. Judges who were blackmailed. It would destroy you."

He turns purple in the face.

I have the faint worry that he might collapse—a heart attack, a stroke. Whatever happens to old people when they completely overload with stress. Then he nods to one of the men, and somehow, through my small experience, I recognize the kill order when it comes.

He's going to kill us here in this loft in the middle of Manhattan, because it's safer than letting the world find out about his crimes. No matter how valuable Elijah is to him, he's more dangerous alive right now. Which means we're dead.

Time slows down, and I look to my right, where the guns sit on the foyer table. White calla lilies and a black titanium gun. *Point and shoot*, he told me. It can't be that simple, but I also have to try. My pulse thumps in my brain like the bass in a club.

I grab the gun. It's lighter than I remember. Or maybe I'm stronger.

Thump. I point and shoot.

Thump. Thump. Red blooms on the lieutenant colonel's uniform.

That's the last thing I see before the world turns upside down...

Elijah flattens me to the ground.

The gun is in his hand instead of mine.

The vase with the calla lilies explodes.

Shards of crystal rain down on us. Elijah pushes me out of the room and down the hall. The world has become eerie and quiet. I can't hear anything, not even my feet pounding down the fire escape.

We make it back to Elijah's car. He buckles me into the passenger seat. Then he's in the driver's seat, and the SUV steers roughly onto the street.

He's shouting something at me, but I can't hear him. His lips are moving. I watch them to see what he's saying. *Stay with me. Stay awake.*

Why would I fall asleep at a time like this? I look down at my body.

Blood spreading across white fabric. Black text stark across my chest. I don't feel any pain. I don't feel anything at all.

THE END

Thank you so much for reading GOLD MINE! I hope you loved this dark and dangerous story. You can order SILVER LINING, the conclusion to Elijah and Holly's story right now...

Elijah North has survived starvation and torture. Now he faces his darkest challenge: the possibility of life without Holly Frank. The woman he loves hangs in the balance. The family he found mourns in the distance. And the future he built crumbles in the wind.

And if you loved reading about Liam North and the violin prodigy he has custody of, you can read OVERTURE right now. Forbidden fruit has never tasted so sweet...

Joshua North also has a book. You can find these books on Amazon, Apple Books, Barnes & Noble, Kobo and wherever books are sold.

Keep reading for an excerpt from OVERTURE...

REST, LIAM TOLD me.

He's right about a lot of things. Maybe he's right about this. I climb onto the cool pink sheets, hoping that a nap will suddenly make me content with this quiet little life.

Even though I know it won't.

Besides, I'm too wired to actually sleep. The white lace coverlet is both delicate and comfy. It's actually what I would have picked out for myself, except I didn't pick it out. I've been incapable of picking anything, of choosing anything, of deciding anything as part of some deep-seated fear that I'll be abandoned.

The coverlet, like everything else in my life, simply appeared.

And the person responsible for its appearance? Liam North.

I climb under the blanket and stare at the ceiling. My body feels overly warm, but it still feels good to be tucked into the blankets. The blankets *he* picked out for me.

It's really so wrong to think of him in a sexual way. He's my guardian, literally. Legally. And he has never done anything to make me think he sees *me* in a sexual way.

This is it. This is the answer.

I don't need to go skinny-dipping in the lake down the hill. Thinking about Liam North in a sexual way is my fast car. My parachute out of a plane.

My eyes squeeze shut.

That's all it takes to see Liam's stern expression, those fathomless green eyes and the glint of dark blond whiskers that are always there by late afternoon. And then there's the way he touched me. My forehead, sure, but it's more than he's done before. That broad palm on my sensitive skin.

My thighs press together. They want something between them, and I give them a pillow. Even the way I masturbate is small and timid, never making a sound, barely moving at all, but I can't change it now. I can't moan or throw back my head even for the sake of rebellion.

But I can push my hips against the pillow, rocking my whole body as I imagine Liam doing more than touching my forehead. He would trail his hand down my cheek, my neck, my shoulder.

Repressed. I'm so repressed it's hard to imagine more than that.

I make myself do it, make myself trail my hand down between my breasts, where it's warm and velvety soft, where I imagine Liam would know exactly how to touch me.

You're so beautiful, he would say. *Your breasts are perfect.*

Because Imaginary Liam wouldn't care about big breasts. He would like them small and soft with pale nipples. That would be the absolute perfect pair of breasts for him.

And he would probably do something obscene and rude. Like lick them.

My hips press against the pillow, almost pushing it down to the mattress, rocking and rocking. There's not anything sexy or graceful about what I'm doing. It's pure instinct. Pure need.

The beginning of a climax wraps itself around me. Claws sink into my skin. There's almost certain death, and I'm fighting, fighting, fighting for it with the pillow clenched hard.

"Oh fuck."

The words come soft enough someone else might not hear them. They're more exhalation of breath, the consonants a faint break in the sound. I have excellent hearing. Ridiculous, crazy good hearing that had me tuning instruments before I could ride a bike.

My eyes snap open, and there's Liam, standing there, frozen. Those green eyes locked on mine. His body clenched tight only three feet away from me. He doesn't come closer, but he doesn't leave.

Orgasm breaks me apart, and I cry out in surprise and denial and relief. "*Liam.*"

It goes on and on, the terrible pleasure of it. The wrenching embarrassment of coming while looking into the eyes of the man who raised me for the past six years.

My hips pump against the mattress, pulling out the last few pulses between my legs.

And then I'm lying there, wrapped tight around a pillow, unable to move, panting.

I've never seen Liam looking anything other than calm and cool and capable. He can handle anything with a command that's almost terrifying in its competency. Right now he looks at a loss.

His voice is low and rough. "We should talk about this."

I can't think of anything in the world I'd rather do less. "Or we could just..." I hate that I still somehow sound breathy and turned on. There are little quivers in my thighs. "Pretend this never happened?"

"Come downstairs when you're—"

The sentence hangs between us, leaving me to fill in the blank. *Come downstairs when you're done fucking yourself in the bed I bought for you. Come downstairs when you're done humiliating yourself.*

He gives a short nod, as if the unspoken answer is the right one.

Then he turns, an about-face appropriate to any military ceremony.

Alone in the room I have no choice but to face the mechanics of untangling myself. Unclenching my fists from the pillow. Pulling apart my legs. Acknowledging the dampness between my thighs.

"Please be a dream," I whisper, but my face is too hot. Burning up. This is real.

Want to read more? Order OVERTURE from Amazon, Barnes & Noble, Apple Books, or Kobo.

Books by Skye Warren

Endgame Trilogy & more books in Tanglewood

The Pawn

The Knight

The Castle

The King

The Queen

Escort

Survival of the Richest

The Evolution of Man

The Bishop

Mating Theory

North Security Trilogy & more North brothers

Overture

Concerto

Sonata

Audition

Chicago Underground series

Rough

Hard

Fierce

Wild

Dirty

Secret

Sweet

Deep

Stripped series

Tough Love

Love the Way You Lie

Better When It Hurts

Even Better

Pretty When You Cry

Caught for Christmas

Hold You Against Me

To the Ends of the Earth

Standalone Dangerous Romance

Wanderlust

On the Way Home

Hear Me

For a complete listing of Skye Warren books, visit

www.skyewarren.com/books

About the Author

Skye Warren is the New York Times bestselling author of dangerous romance such as the Endgame trilogy. Her books have been featured in Jezebel, Buzzfeed, USA Today Happily Ever After, Glamour, and Elle Magazine. She makes her home in Texas with her loving family, sweet dogs, and evil cat.

Sign up for Skye's newsletter:
www.skyewarren.com/newsletter

Like Skye Warren on Facebook:
facebook.com/skyewarren

Join Skye Warren's Dark Room reader group:
skyewarren.com/darkroom

Follow Skye Warren on Instagram:
instagram.com/skyewarrenbooks

Visit Skye's website for her current booklist:
www.skyewarren.com

COPYRIGHT

Gold Mine © 2020 by Skye Warren
Print Edition

Cover design by Book Beautiful
Formatted by BB Ebooks

www.ingramcontent.com/pod-product-compliance
Lightning Source LLC
Chambersburg PA
CBHW050312110726
47899CB00007B/2216